Although Storme Knight is a newlywed, she dearly wants to have their first child sooner rather than later. She's stood on her head—literally—to become pregnant. But despite using no birth control, how well she eats, rests, and makes love, her attempts fail.

Craig Knight wants a child someday. With COVID-19 still raging, the purchase of his own law firm, and virtually no money in their bank account, having a baby isn't his first priority. He thinks a baby will come with time and is in no particular hurry to take on any additional expenses.

Storme feels differently and will do *anything* to get pregnant. When Sunny, with her wacky plans, offers to help, how can a desperate Storme refuse? What could possibly go wrong?

Mountain Due

ISBN: 978-1-4874-3245-4
Cover art by Martine Jardin

Published by eXtasy Books Inc or
Devine Destinies, an imprint of eXtasy Books Inc

Look for us online at:
www.eXtasybooks.com or www.devinedestinies.com

Mountain Due
Mountain Series 15

By

Kathy Kalmar

DEDICATION

To Larry, who gave me my very own second chance to love, more happiness than I could have believed possible, and healed three broken hearts in the process. I swear I can't love you any more than I already do, and the next day proves me wrong.

In Memoriam

To my forever friend, Linda Wilson, whose skills, talents, and belief in me and my work led to this publication and every book I write. Ours is a relationship forged in the fires of pain, loss, love and laughter. Living without you is very difficult.

To Ron Wilson, my best friend, who got me through the best and more importantly, the worst times in my life with his insight, sense of humor, loyalty, and friendship. He thought I could do anything I've ever wanted to do, and he was right.

Acknowledgment

For Carolyn Gilbreath, her counsel and encouragement made this a better book. She is my Best Friend Forever and Beta reader and coplotter extraordinaire.

And with great gratitude, I acknowledge Jay Austin, extraordinary Editor in Chief; Debbie Nygaard, super-editor; Martine Jardin, artist; Brigit Vries, Assistant Editor in Chief; The Greater Detroit Romance Writers of America; and you, my readers. For Doug Marple, webmaster, who keeps the social media site wheels turning. I'm grateful to you all.

Disclaimer. Any medical mistakes herein are mine. Currently COVID-19 is still infecting the United States. The treatments mentioned reflect the ever-changing information available at this time. Hopefully, an effective vaccine will work efficiently.

CHAPTER ONE: CAN'T STOP THE FEELING

Sunny Days barreled through the doors of her twin sister's mountain view home while she balanced the pizza she'd picked up curbside for their lunch. "Yoo-hoo! Storme, where are you?"

Craig snatched a piece as he walked out the door. Sunny fought to catch her balance when he did as the pizza shifted from opening the box top. She used both hands to steady it, then once it stabilized, she wiped a hand over her sweating brow. "Phew."

She found her sister in bed on her back, still in her pajamas. Her hands supported her hips while her legs pointed skyward, a pillow—beneath her.

Sunny stood with her hands on her hips, shaking her head. "Girl, we need to talk about this yoga craze of yours."

Storme just grunted in response. "Go away."

"That's a strange way to do yoga. Don't you need a firm surface and a yoga mat or something? I've never seen that position before. What's it called? Bats in the Belfry?" she teased. "Are you sure you want me to take a hike? I brought lunch."

Storme grumbled, "What are you doing here?" She slowly lowered herself into a more normal position and licked her lips when she inhaled the intoxicating aroma of the famous tomato sauce and artesian cheeses. Ski Mountain Pizza was *thee* best pizza ever.

Sunny rolled her eyes. "Duh. What's it look like? I brought my hermit sister a mouthwatering pizza."

Storme turned her head, her sky-blue eyes glaring. Her lips

formed a thin line. "It looks like you're tempting fate again, going out like this."

Sunny shrugged her shoulders. "Fine. Be that way. I'll eat it by myself." She turned to leave. "Lockdown's been lifted since Memorial Day, and all the tourists are out and about, and they're fine."

Storme carefully lowered her legs to climb off the round bed, trying to block Sunny's escape. "My point exactly. No one knows whether or not they're asymptomatic. Few wear masks. The pandemic is not *over* just because it's summer. By the way, thanks for springing for the pizza. We're penny-pinching lately."

"I'm your twin sister. We catch things together. Remember chicken pox?"

Storme backed away from her. "Wait. Do you think you have—"

"Of course not! I'm careful. I'm not yanking your chain, or at least I haven't yet." She removed her facemask decorated with tiny pink man parts. "So, no risk, right? I wear my mask, as you can see, but you haven't answered my question. What were you doing with your legs sky high?"

Storme threw her a look and grimaced. "Trying to get preggers. Keep those little swimmers headed to my baby-maker." Tears welled in her eyes and threatened to overfill and spill down her cheeks.

Sunny could see how much Storme yearned for a baby. The tears running down her identical twin's face made that perfectly clear as they headed for the kitchen.

Sunny set the pizza down on the marble island in the white farmhouse kitchen and took a big bite of the yummy, fragrant pizza. They moved to the Great Room with its million-dollar view of the mountains, which displayed a verdant green space of every hue imaginable. The floor-to-ceiling windows showed the Smoky Mountains at their majestic best. All the negative ions released from the surrounding evergreens should provide all the necessary energy she needed to embark on this life-changing quest.

Storme joined her and snagged a piece of pizza drenched in wonderful gooey cheese. "Mm good. This pizza is to die for."

Sunny blew on her fingernails and buffed them against her t-shirt. "I know, right? But do I have to have *the talk* with you again? Let me be clear here. I repeat . . . That's not how you make a baby."

Storme lips made a pout. "I know, but I don't have the help from the legendary Ghost Stag and his magic to ensure a pregnancy like you and Jesse do. Craig and I have been trying . . . and no baby . . . nothing."

Sunny lifted a brow. "You haven't been married all that long, ya know. Maybe you're expecting too much, too soon."

Storme swallowed her bite of pizza, took a swig of cider from the Apple Barn Cider Mill Complex in Sevierville, and said slowly, "Easy for you to say. You're all but destined to get pregnant by year's end cuz that's how the legend goes, but the only stag I have in my corner is Craig. What if there's something wrong with his equipment?" She swallowed hard. "Or mine?"

Sunny shrugged. "Don't go there. You have no reason to. I'm loose as a goose, and if you relaxed, you would probably get pregnant."

"Well, Dr. Google said after you have sex, raise your legs to help those swimmers reach your uterus and let gravity help suck it in there. I told you that."

Sunny laughed. "For reals? I thought you were joshin'."

"Yup. I've been Googling fertility, and that's what it says, *raise your hips for fifteen to twenty minutes after sex*."

"Does Craig know you're trying to get pg?"

"Well, if he doesn't, he's certainly not complaining. We're

not using protection. By now, he should know the birds and the bees and all that jazz."

Sunny frowned. "Okay. I get it. I'll help in any way I can. Operation Baby is a go. I call dibs on being the Godmother."

Storme's mouth gaped open. "Okeydokey. Really? You get it? You're in? You'll help me?"

After an eye roll, Sunny growled, "I just said I would."

"All right, Operation Baby, it is." Storme giggled. "For once, I don't mind your operation fascination."

Sunny winked. "I should have named it Mission Mommy." She smiled, knowing her *say-so* should provide the confidence that no task was too great for her plans. "Once I begin a mission, I never surrender. You know how I am. You want a baby? We'll get you a baby. But we should really bring Mom in on this. And probably Dr. Cyd. If anyone knows about babies, it's those two."

Storme looked a tad bit wary. "Good thinking. You think Mom will suggest cannabis?"

Sunny winked. "I sure hope so. That'll relax you. Both Mom and Dr. Cyd use homeopathic medicine, so they must know something. Mom was older than us when she had Skye. We're young. You're probably fertile as a turtle."

A gleam appeared in Storme's gaze, and hope eclipsed the tears Sunny had seen when she arrived with the pizza.

Storme straightened her shoulders. She swallowed hard and cleared her throat. "All righty then."

"Yahoo! Now you're talkin', sista. You need to clear this with Craig, ya know. Just saying. He is a mere male. He should understand what we're actually doing. Meanwhile, let's see what we can find out about your best chances to grow a mini you. Maybe I should call it Mission Mini-Me."

Storme nodded. "You goof. Yeah, you're right, though. Connecting the dots may be expecting too much from Craig. He probably just likes ridin' bareback and isn't really thinking about a baby." She took another piece of pizza. "Since I might be eating for two, I'm chowing down. Who knows?"

Sunny tapped her chest. "I know, and I say there are several ways to get pregnant, ya know."

Storme pouted. "The good old-fashioned way hasn't done it. I'm so desperate, I'll try *anything*. Even listening to you."

Sunny growled and became outraged. "I thought you wanted my help."

Storme's nod was vigorous. "I do. Really."

"Okeydokey. Good. I have several plans. Some you'll like. Some you won't. I'll be right back. There's something I want to get first. If a picture's worth a thousand words, then the real deal ought to do the trick." She rummaged through Storme's farmhouse-decor kitchen drawers. "Ta-da! Here it is." She grabbed an item, held it behind her, and approached her twin.

Storme's wary gaze still looked unconvinced. "What kitchen item can help? You better not have found an egg. That would be *so* not funny."

Sunny threw her a *come on now* look. "Duh. That was a lame play on words, ya know. Get a gander of this." She brandished a turkey baster.

Storme burst out laughing. "I'm not gonna shove that thing up my va-jay-jay."

"No, seriously. It's truly called the Turkey Baster Method. It's a real thing."

"Is not."

"Is too." Sunny grabbed Storme's computer and Googled it, showing her it was a bona fide alternative method. Although the image showed a plunger syringe rather than the baster she held. "You said you'll try anything."

"Next, you'll be suggesting a tried-and-true Twin Switch." Storme put her hand over her mouth, obviously praying she hadn't said that out loud.

Sunny said, "Hmm, if it calls for that . . ."

Storme looked far from convinced.

Sunny noticed her uncertainty. "So shoot me. Don't use my help." She spun on her heel and made to leave.

Storme reached out to stop her. "Not so fast, Sunny. Let me think."

Sunny paused. "That's more like it. Let's brainstorm."

Storme took a breath. "Brainstorming is my fav way to plan." She grabbed a pen and paper, handed them to her, and reclaimed the laptop.

Holly, Storme's Christmas kitten, loved to curl up onto the warm laptop whenever Storme was using it. Holly demanded her share of attention and did what she could to try to keep Storme off the computer, especially batting at the keyboard. Storme shooed her off with her hands but bent to kiss and fondle her first.

Sunny always thought better with a pen between her fingers, and her twin knew that, so she kept a steno pad and pen nearby.

"No idea is too radical." She nodded and thought for a minute. "I'll start with Mom and her apothecary skills, too. Her input could be helpful."

"I dunno . . . Don't forget Dr. Cyd."

Sunny gave Storme the shame-shame gesture. "Breaking the brainstorm rules already? No idea is wrong. I thought you wanted a baby."

"I do. Now, don't get used to this, but . . . you're right."

Sunny puffed her chest out. "I know. I usually am. Right, that is, in case you forgot. I'm usually right about these things in life, but does anyone believe me? Nooo. Y'all think I'm a space cadet. Truth is, I think faster than the rest of you. How about IVF, in vitro fertilization?"

"If you say so. Thus far, we have IVF, Mom, Dr. Cyd . . ."

Sunny snapped her fingers. "Our half-sister, Dawn. She's a

nurse, and she's still assigned to the Lodge during this pandemic. She must know something useful. I'm drawing a blank. Fresh out of ideas. We need Dr. Google. Where's the laptop?"

Storme lifted it. "Right here, remember?" She opened it and Googled *fertility, conception, and pregnancy. Diet* came up, and she followed the links and leads those sites provided. "There's acupuncture." She shuddered. "Needles. Ugh. But write it down."

"You write it down."

"I'm on the computer. You're the writer. Don't be cute with me."

"Diet. Did you hear that?" Sunny prompted as she added it to her handwritten list.

Storme added *diet* to the computer version. "Drugs. I hate that one, but . . ."

Sunny straightened in her chair. "Taking your temperature and tracking ovulation."

"Sounds like a hassle to me."

Sunny cocked her brow. "No judgments now. Surrogacy."

Storme started to protest.

Sunny held up a hand and sing-songed, "Breaking the brainstorming rules again."

"Self-impregnation. What's that?"

Sunny shrugged her shoulders. "Dunno. We'll look into that later. What else?"

Storme's brow made a deep V. "We're scraping the bottom of the barrel as it is here."

"Storme Marie Knight, you are *so* not patient. We're not done yet."

Storme nodded. "Ya got that right, at least. I do want a baby . . . like *yesterday*! At the latest." She grinned. "Keep talking."

Sunny exclaimed, "Exercise."

"Huh?"

Sunny reached over and pointed at the display on the computer screen. "That's what it says. I can read it from here. How'd you miss it? Must be a Freudian thing. I know how you hate exercising. "

Storme nodded. "Hormones and herbs are right next to that data. I'll click on that."

"Oh, look, what about a sperm donor?"

Storme's nose wrinkled, as did her forehead. "How about an egg donor?"

"I'll add it."

"Nuts." Storme giggled.

"Very funny."

"No, seriously. That's what this says. Actually, walnuts, but nuts are nuts, right? Write down legumes. They're not nuts, but they make the good-for-fertility list and suchlike."

Sunny added that to their growing list. "Okay. Artificial insemination."

"We kinda covered that, but I'll record that. No birth control."

Sunny rolled her eyes. "Duh! Geesh. So much for Captain Obvious. Add no caffeine to your list."

"Yikes! No Mountain Dew, tea, or coffee?"

Sunny grimaced. "Worse, no chocolate."

"Hold on a minute. Chocolate comes from beans. Beans are vegetables, so chocolate is a veggie."

Sunny giggled. "There's a caffeine-free version."

Storme shrugged. "What's the point then? It's the jolt I like."

Sunny grinned. "Just sayin'. Maintain a healthy weight."

Storme looked up in surprise. "But I'll be eating for two."

"Not anymore. Maybe back when Gram was pregnant, but not in 2020."

"Killjoy. Take Folic Acid."

Sunny laughed. "Hell, no acid for me. Remember what it did to Dad?"

It was Storme's turn to giggle. "Not that acid! Next you'll say fruits and veggies!"

"You must be psychic."

Storme continued. "No soy. Yikes, Chinese food without soy sauce? Heresy."

Sunny glanced back at the computer. "Hmm, no processed foods."

"Bye-bye bacon-covered hot dogs."

"Who eats that?"

"Craig."

"Not anymore, he doesn't. It says right here most of this applies to the father-to-be, too."

Storme continued her Google search. "Avoid trans fats. Hell, all the goodies are gone!"

Sunny looked up. "Real mature. Are you sure you're really mom material?"

"Since when did you get so mature? Today's the day you decided to grow up and be an adult?"

Sunny smacked her. "Eat things with vitamin C, E, and B."

"There's my case for chocolate-covered raisins. I bet they have both."

"I seriously doubt that, but get your ZZZs."

"Now, that I can do."

"Can't smoke."

"Get serious. Neither of us do that. Not since Luke said we held a cigarette like a man. Seriously, it's hard to stop *being* smokin'. I'm already smokin' hot, according to Craig. No can do."

"Hardee-har-har."

Sunny continued their Google search and read, "Skip alcohol. That means no butterscotch moonshine."

"Bummer." Storme frowned. "But apple moonshine is

okay, right? It's made from fruits and veggies. Corn and apples."

"That's a stretch."

Storme yawned and stretched. "No, what I just did was a stretch. That no moonshine thingy is cruel and unusual punishment."

"This will cheer you up. Different positions for sex."

"Now that's what I'm talking about!" they said in unison with gusto.

Storme shifted her body into a more comfortable position, squiggling her back, neck, and shoulders. "Enough already. I'm tired. Let's scan the list into the computer. I'll email it to you. Use red ink or another color to add to it when you have a chance, and I'll do the same. I need a nap."

"No nap for you, missy. You need to walk off the pizza. Exercise, remember? Oh, by the way, you'll need protein but not too much dairy. Dairy impacts fertility—for both you and Craig."

Storme nodded. "I like it when what good for the goose . . ."

" . . . is good for the gander." Sunny finished and laughed with her sister. "Get dressed and get moving. We're walking past Chestnut to Wiley Oakley."

"That's too far, and it's uphill."

Sunny put her hands on her hips. "If you're not ready to do what you need to do, you're not ready for no baby, sista."

Storme grumbled. "Oh? And you're so mature, huh?"

Sunny wagged her finger in warning. "Hey there, hold on a minute. I'll have you know I raised two kids."

"Did not."

"Did too. Ashe and Ashley. To adulthood. Look how good they turned out."

"They're goats, Sunny.

"*Kid* goats. Kids are kids. Still counts."

"Does not."

"Does too."

Storme headed to her bedroom to change. She came back wearing jean shorts and an oversized top. "Tell you what, I'll walk Edgewood."

Sunny beamed.

"As long as you do, too."

Sunny deflated.

"What? Backing out now? You said"—she made air quotes—"*we're in this together. I'll help.*"

Sunny grimaced in protest. "Not *that* much together, but I am gonna help. By the way, Edgewood passes Chestnut. You're on."

"Shit! I forgot about that section. I was thinking of walking *to* Woodland from Edgewood."

"We could do that Wiley-Oakley-Edgewood loop. Just sayin'."

"No way, Jose. I'll walk from the house to Woodland and back. Then I'm catching those ZZZs you were talking about."

"We should think about filling Craig in while we walk," Sunny suggested.

"That requires some planning."

"Now, yer talkin'. Scheming is what we do best."

Sunny play-bumped her sister's side as they moved down the walkway onto the road lined with a variety of young hardwoods that had sprung up since the wildfire. Fireweed sprouted first and made a pretty contrast to the green trees growing on either side of the road. The breeze in the air seemed to bless them and their plans.

Craig Knight was worried. He was also exhausted. COVID-19 had made serious inroads into his law practice income.

Shortly after reconnecting with Storme, he'd bought his father's business. His dad was cool with their arrangement and had given him a break with the terms of purchase. Still, neither of them foresaw the economic effects the coronavirus created. Even his father's success and savings could only carry him so far. Times were tough for everyone. *Dad deserves to enjoy his golden years. He doesn't need me to drain him.*

Thus far, Craig had managed to keep making the payments, but things had yet to return to normal. Although divorce statistics were up since the forced shutdown, folks didn't have the money to file paperwork. Plus the courts were slow to open when summer arrived. Fortunately, there were positive aspects to the corporate side of things as new companies tried to start up in the ever-changing needs of Gatlinburg. Businesses came and went with the tourist flow. There were still mergers and buyouts, but much of his time was spent on bankruptcy claims. Obviously, there wasn't a lot of money in those transactions.

When he tried to sleep, his thoughts tossed and turned along with his body. Those thoughts tumbled like dry autumn leaves in the breeze. Maybe he needed more than hot sex with his stunning vixen wife, Storme. *That should wipe me out.* Was it time to get a prescription? Melatonin wasn't cutting it.

He knew Storme wanted a baby, and he did too, but part of him was relieved they didn't have to face that yet. *I am ready for a kid, but the timing's terrible. Storme is unhappy it's taking so long. We've only been married since Christmas . . . and there's a pandemic to worry about. How does being pregnant and a pandemic work? Will she be at greater risk? Seems likely.* He frowned, hating to disappoint her. He supported their efforts, but . . . *Hell, who am I kidding? I love the making a baby part, but we can't afford one now.* He left the office and began the short drive home.

As he pulled off Wiley Oakley onto Woodland, he spied Storme and her twin with their heads together as they walked in the road. *Uh-oh. Trouble usually erupts when those two conspire. What shitstorm awaits me now?*

He tooted his horn in greeting and didn't feel any better when they pulled apart to wave. An unease unrelated to his financial concerns filled him. Not with dread exactly—okay, exactly with dread, filling his knotting stomach. His gut told him something was up, but what? God only knew. He and his brother-in-law, Jesse, often felt they were living with the latest incarnation of Lucy and Ethel from the back-in-the-day television show, *I Love Lucy. Something has them talking up a storm.*

He pulled his monster pickup truck into the forty-five-degree driveway, set the emergency brake, and grabbed his laptop and briefcase. He looked around as he walked up the concrete path to their round-shaped house. *Glad I upgraded and leveled this path after Storme fell, breaking her leg and wrist. That accident led to our Christmas wedding a year later.* A smile came to his face as he recalled those fateful days. *I didn't want her, or any kids we have, to suffer a similar incident. The house is big enough for kids. Won't take much to change a bedroom into a nursery. Wow, I'm thinking like a—dare I put it into words?—a Dad.*

He got out of the car, automatically locking it so no trickster bear could get inside as they often did nowadays. The bears were taking back their habitat after the 2016 Wildfire. They kept a close eye on their cat, Holly, as she lazed on the deck that circled their house, even though these black bears weren't carnivores. Bobcats were another story, though, and they had also moved back into the area.

Holly, with her red and green collar and silver bell tinkling as she walked, wound her way through his legs as he entered the house. She purred loudly. *It's like even the cat is buttering me up, but for what?*

He didn't have long to wait for Storme to enter the house and plant a hot wet kiss that made him want to head for their bedroom and make long, sweet love. He felt himself rise to the occasion and was surprised she didn't lead him that way.

Instead, she said, "Save that fire for the grill. We're having chicken, baked potatoes, and a nice leafy, green salad." Then she headed for the kitchen.

What's up with her? Usually she's up for some nookie, too. He entered the bedroom, shed his suit coat, and changed into cargo shorts and a t-shirt.

After what could only be described as a stormy courtship and a crazy-ass wedding, Storme was finally his wife. He had his practice and a cute-as-hell cat that had once carried his engagement ring on her collar. And despite COVID-19 and its threat to his newly acquired in-laws, life was good. *So why am I on guard?*

Storme was setting the deck table for their dinner and humming a song that nagged at his memory. It was a golden oldie. But what was it? He snapped his fingers. *Having my Baby* by Paul Anka. *Could she be . . .* He looked at his wife closely.

Her body was fit and trim. The only bumps he saw were her breasts, which she called *Bo* and *Peep*. He shook his head. A smile crossed his face, and he chuckled. It was one of the things he loved most about her. She named everything—plants, bears, and body parts. She called her pussy *Virginia*—when she didn't use va-jay-jay like Oprah—because it once was a virgin.

He grabbed the marinating chicken and went to the grill to cook it. He shook his head as he thought about when her period came. She called it Bloody Mary. *Speaking of which, isn't it due pretty soon? Time flies, and she doesn't keep track – does she? I don't think she's very regular, and with her bookkeeping background, that irks the hell out of her. Seems like each period has been a surprise.* He paused a moment, the chicken breast still held in the claws of the tongs, and thought about her recent reactions. *Maybe each period represented a missed chance to conceive? Were her mini bouts of depression really disappointment?* He shook those thoughts out of his head. *It's not like me to think of stuff like periods. The less I know, the better. Maybe we should bury the bone tonight if she's gonna start soon. Won't have a chance otherwise.*

The coals were ready, so he put the chicken on the grill. After he pushed the potatoes deep within the briquettes, his thoughts turned to *pushing* his hardening cock inside *Storme's* heat.

Wisely, Storme kept the salad inside until they were ready to eat. He hoped Monday, the black bear—known to frequent their mountain every Monday—wouldn't show up hungry for dinner to disturb theirs.

Holly followed Storme out when he announced that dinner was ready, no doubt hoping for a handout.

Storme tossed the salad with homemade dressing her mother whipped up. He could swear it held traces of rose and lavender. No doubt Marsha had added her famous cannabis. He no longer asked, preferring not to dwell on the legalities of it. Whenever he pressed Marsha on the topic, she'd say she pleaded the 5th. He knew it was supposed to be CBD, cannabidiol, and he hoped that was correct. But Storme usually didn't use Marsha's products with him. *Why am I so suspicious all of a sudden? At most, it'll relax us and cheer us up, so what's my deal?* Still, the attorney in him sat up and took notice, but Storme didn't seem particularly concerned.

His spidey senses went on full alert when she began to talk baby again. "What were you and Sunny so busy talking about when I drove in?"

"We were talking about the legend of the Ghost Stag."

"The soulmate thing?"

"No, the baby thing."

Craig stopped chewing. "Say what?"

"Remember if you see it, the couple is supposed to conceive before the year is up?"

Craig nodded. "Yes."

"Well, our joint anniversary comes in December, remember?"

"How could I ever forget our double Snowmageddon Christmas weddin'?"

She giggled. "That was a surprise, all right. Weren't the bagpipes a great touch for the double ring wedding of the century? What a way to close out 2019."

Craig prompted. "So . . . Ghost Stag?"

"The year is almost up, and we wondered what we'd get for Christmas. Maybe a little package."

Craig coughed suddenly, and his hard cider sprayed on the fist he raised to catch it. "We didn't see the Ghost Stag. *They'll* be the ones expecting."

Storme straightened in her seat and squared her shoulders. "Sunny and I do everything together. We'd like to be preggers together, too. How 'bout you?"

Craig swallowed. "You know I want kids, although December sounds kinda soon."

Storme bristled, and her tone turned sharp and icy. "What if I'm pregnant now?"

Craig stammered as he tried to speak. "Uh . . . I . . . I guess that'd be . . . okay."

Storme rose from the table and began clearing it. "I thought you wanted kids."

He nodded. He did want them. "Are you?"

Frown lines spread across her forehead. "I don't know. I don't think so, anyway. I'd like to be. Are you cool with that?"

He tried to hide his anguished grimace. "I am. Just not today . . ."

The dishes clattered as she hastily gathered them up helter-skelter. A fork fell to the deck, and Holly pounced on it.

Craig tried again. "With COVID-19 and things so unsettled . . . I'd like it to be gone so y'all can be safe."

"Whatever."

Storm strode into the house, and Craig followed. She loaded the dishwasher, not rinsing the plates off first like he preferred. It was a small passive-aggressive maneuver, hopefully only signaling her discontent.

She muttered. "Fine."

What I'd say? What's wrong with the truth? But he knew what was wrong. Storme wanted a baby now, COVID-19 be damned.

Chapter Two: Hang on Sloopy

Storme welcomed Craig when he approached her in bed that night. *Can't get pregnant without him.* Normally, she was really upfront about her feelings. If she was hurt, she cried. When angry, she gave as good as she got, but she wasn't either of those. No, this time she kind of got it.

They did need money, and COVID-19 was now a bona fide pandemic. She was just disappointed. So she didn't feign hard to get and didn't fend him off or pointedly roll away from his careful approach. Instead, she welcomed him. They were good together, in and out of bed. She didn't want to mess that up. Besides, she craved and needed his comfort and the support their lovemaking would provide.

Craig expertly used his hot kisses, his wet mouth, and his hands to convey what words could not. He began slowly—oh, so slowly. When she snuggled into his embrace, he gathered her in closer.

She heard his sigh of relief and contentment, the low groans when he turned her back to his front, and the catch in his breath when her naked hips nestled into his groin. It was impossible to ignore his turgid rod. Her body warmed at his touch. She loved him so much and wanted a piece of their love to show for it—like their baby.

His soft sigh conveyed his delight as his fingers raised shivers along her spine and his mouth dropped feather-light kisses down her back.

She loved the thrills that followed his kisses along the column of her neck. She felt herself moisten at his touch and quivered when he played among the delicate hairs at the apex of her legs. As he nibbled at her ears, shivers raced to replace the thrills he'd caused moments before, and her nipples pebbled and tightened under his feather-light touch. Moans of pleasure escaped when he spun her around and devoured her lips in a hungry kiss.

She went into hyperspace when his mouth moved to each nipple before gently drawing it into his mouth. His tongue drove her closer and closer to the edge.

As delight filled her, all thoughts of anything baby-related fled and flowed straight through the rising tension of her impending climax.

Her fingers twined through his curling locks. He wore his hair a bit shaggy and the stubble that outlined his jaw excited her as it brushed across her body.

Storme had one last coherent thought before she fell over the edge of ecstasy. *I don't care if this is make-up sex or not. It's okay even if we don't make a baby. Trying is fun. But if I do . . .*

As she got her breath under control, she snuggled into Craig's side. She let her fingers traced his firm, full lips, then felt his face relax as she followed his jawline with light kisses. She ran her fingers up and down his taut stomach muscles as if playing Eensy Weensy Spider with light, quick, searching taps that made sure of their mark. Her path went lower, lower, and lower until she reached his throbbing, hard, wet-with-pre-cum cock.

Then she stroked him until he began to pant and his breath caught, indicating his readiness.

She stilled her hand and mounted him. She rode his turgid, hard-as-a-rock length until he gently turned her to lie on her back. She welcomed him inside her and let *him* ride *her*, opening wide to receive him. Her clenching muscles and surrender added to the spasms that brought the magic and release they both craved.

Storme woke up feeling fine as wine until later in the day when she began cramping. By dinnertime, she was spotting. By nightfall, she was flowing. Her period had arrived whether she wanted it or not.

Her spirits lowered like the sails of a boat battened down for a storm. She bent her head and cried in huge gulping sobs. Her shoulders shook with each sob ripping her heart and tearing her very soul to shreds. She felt like a piece of broken glass with each shard piercing her. *It's not fair. I want a baby. So many others conceive unwanted babies, but here I am . . .*

Then she called Sunny.

Her voice shook, and she spoke in a low tone. "Martha is here visiting. The bitch."

"It's a good thing I know what you're talking about. You name everything. I haven't heard that term since I was fourteen. I thought you called it Bloody Mary? Bummer. Don't give up. Now we can begin tracking your periods, figure out when you ovulate, and when you'll be fertile. Buck up, buttercup, and do your research. Eat those fruits and veggies. It won't hurt to get your body ready. Let Bloody Mary Martha get all the toxins out of your system. Then we'll launch our attack."

Storme shrugged, knowing her twin couldn't see her movement. "Craig is not as ready as we are. I didn't tell him about Operation Baby, but we did talk about having a baby."

Sunny's tone sharpened. "And?"

Storme ground out, "He countered with, money, the right time . . . Yadda, yadda, yadda." Her voice rose with her worry. "What if he doesn't want one?"

"Don't be silly. Look at him with Skye's brood. He's a natural for *dadhood*. Besides, there is no *right* time. Look at Mom and Mariah. You get pregnant whenever the Fates decide. Ready or not, money or not."

"Easy for you to say. You have Ghost Stag magic working for you."

"There's always adoption and IVF."

"That takes money, honey, and we don't have much since Craig started the process to buy his father out. And oh, yeah, COVID-19 shut down the courts and turned off the economy."

"There's such a thing as a Mosie."

Storme's tone rose an octave. "What the fuck is that?"

"Whoa, sista. You getting' all menstrual bitchy. It's a mini turkey baster. Actually, it's a fancy-dancy syringe thingy. All you need is this syringe, trademarked Mosie, and sperm, and voila, you're preggers. You can get one online. Maybe you should see Dr. Cyd or your gynecologist."

"Cyd's a good idea. Doc Waters said I may have a touch of endometritis, and I should have some hysterosalpingography or sumthin' else I can't spell or pronounce. Plus, other expensive, invasive tests for which I have no money, time, or desire. I mean *ick*, poke around down there inside of me? I don't think so."

"Oh, what's that quack know? You don't need all that. We just need some eggs and sperm. You have eggs. He has sperm."

She swallowed past the lump in her throat. "And I got my period." She swiped at her tears.

Sunny's tone was bracing and sure. "Okay, so do your research. Eat right. Buck up."

"You're getting redundant."

"You are."

They giggled, and Storme grabbed a hot pad and an afghan and lay on the blood-red leather couch to run a computer search as she endured her unwanted period. The more she read, the more overwhelmed she got. She learned about ovulation kits and basal temperature, ovulation, ovulation tests, x-ray contrasts, ovarian reserve and imaging tests, and laparoscopy surgery. None of it appealed to her. It sounded terrible and depressing. Nonetheless, she added it all to their rapidly expanding brainstorming list, shut the laptop down, and took a nap.

When she woke up, she called Dr. Cyd Garden to facetime with her. Dr. Cyd conducted her practice from her home on Airport Road near Marsha's Mellow Magic Apothecary. Storme laid out her case.

Cyd listened closely, watching on her phone's screen. When Storme finished, she asked. "You're what, about twenty-five? Twenty-six?"

"Yup."

"That's young enough. You've been trying since you married, right? Correct me if I'm wrong, but that's not even a year ago. I suggest that you practice yoga and meditation along with dietary additions. You can think about acupuncture to clear any blocked chakras. In the meantime, I'll email you some smoothie recipes for you and Craig that can help boost fertility. Your mother can help you find the basics. Use almond, not dairy milk. Dairy negatively affects fertility, so avoid cheese, too. Check your vaginal secretions. When they are clear, copious, wet, and slippery, you'll be ovulating. Have sex every other day but don't overdo the newlywed sex. In the meantime, stop the paralysis by analysis."

Storme's forehead creased. "Stop what?"

Dr. Cyd chuckled. "Stop overwhelming yourself with TMI, too much information, so badly that you can't make a move."

Storme giggled.

"And call your Mom. She has a knack for this kind of thing."

"Thanks, Dr. Cyd. I think."

"Stop thinking. Start shopping for chai seeds, fresh figs, goji berries, and bee pollen."

"Yuck. I don't know where to begin."

Dr. Cyd responded in a firmer tone. "Call your mother. Bye, now."

Storme added Cyd's info to the list and started a new one—a shopping list. She longed for the day when she could add strollers and baby blankets to it.

Chapter Three: Practice Makes Perfect

Storme decided that an ovulation kit wouldn't be too invasive and would help them know the best time to make love that should ultimately result in a baby. From what she'd read, the kit would use her urine to detect a hormone whose levels increased each month during ovulation. The hormone caused the ovaries to release an egg. The three days right after a positive test result were the best times for them to have sex to achieve conception. She figured that was about mid-way through her menstrual cycle. She also discovered that Dr. Cyd was right. The slippery nature of her vaginal fluids during that time would help Craig's swimmers reach her egg. *Decidedly worth the moola, her time, and a trip to the drugstore in town. Can't hurt. Afterward, I'll stop in to see Mom, give her my list, and see what she can do. Gotta try something, and sometimes that's my mother, even though she's a whole 'nother other.* She grinned. She had an Action Plan. Operation Baby was activated and provided her with marching orders.

By lunchtime, Storme was entering Mellow Magic Apothecary. Marsha's long curly salt and pepper hair was tied back with a strip of leather with feathers attached to the ends. She wore an off-the-shoulders hemp top with a retro psychedelic print. Her gathered skirt flowed below the deerskin twist she used as a belt. Leather bracelets with beads covered both wrists. Sandalwood incense wafted in the air, blending with dried lavender, rose petals, and jasmine. CeCe McWilliams, the local artist who'd painted the Ghost Stag canvas on display at the Lodge, was behind the glass showcase counters, obviously helping out.

A huge smile creased Marsha's face upon seeing Storme. She rushed over, gathered her in her arms, and asked, "How can I help you?"

"What makes you think I need help?"

"Well, for starters, that gleam in your eye and that paper in your hand. Doesn't take a rocket scientist to figure out." She took the list from her and noted, "Goji berries, dried fig, chia seeds, chasteberry, raspberry leaf tea . . . I see."

From the glint in Marsha's gaze, she had obviously put two and two together. She handed the list to CeCe. "Add some cinnamon sticks, ginger root, passionflower, and pomegranate powder to that order, will you?"

Marsha then directed Storme outside to sit beside the stream that ran behind the apothecary. The music of the stream tripping over stones in its way relaxed Storme.

"Tell Mama all about it. Spill." Maternal command was in Marsha's tone.

To Storme's horror, tears splashed down her face like the stream making its way to a waterfall. "I don't know what's wrong with me."

"I'd bet you're menstrual."

"How'd you know?"

"I know my daughter. You've made no bones about wanting to become a mother. So what else could it be? If you and Craig were on the outs, you'd be red hot mad, but you're sad. It's more than menstrual hormones, but we can navigate this." Marsha winked. "Your list tells me you've been in touch with Cyd. She also suggested a smoothie with almond milk, right? We often join forces to help women conceive. There's a number of things we can do to stimulate conception in addition to my potions."

"I just may need one of those things if this doesn't work."

Marsha's laughter bubbled. "Methinks you don't need a love potion."

"I may need a spell or something to get Craig to fully get on board with the baby thing."

Marsha nodded. "Most men don't set out to make babies when they make love. Takes 'em time to get the father thing. Actually, your visit isn't surprising. Sunny was here yesterday—"

"What?" Storme gathered herself and huffed. "Is that how you knew?"

"Settle your feathers. I said this wasn't rocket science. Your shopping list, remember? Sunny was interested in potions."

"Not again."

"Not this time. She asked for a forgetting potion."

Storme screeched. "What the hell!"

Marsha lifted her hands, palms upwards, and shrugged. "She said something about a Spanish fly, too."

"OMG! Who and what does she want forgotten? She didn't say anything about switching identities, did she?"

Marsha's response was slow. "I don't think so. She wouldn't go that far, would she? I mean, would she drug you? Craig? Both of you? All I know is she asked. She's trying to help, she said. What's she talking about?"

Storme ground her teeth and took a deep breath. "We were brainstorming how I can get pregnant . . ."

"That's easy. Make love."

"I have been . . . we have been, but I'm not pregnant. Sunny has the magic of the Ghost Stag, so inadvertently, I mentioned a Twin Switch. I took it back right away, but you know Sunny. Obviously, that's where she went."

Marsha laughed. "It's not the worst idea. People have done that. You *do* share identical DNA, so she'd be a perfect surrogate."

Storme shrugged. "I know. All we need is Craig's sperm."

Marsha looked like she got the drift. "So, let me get this straight. Sunny's jumped way ahead and decided the best option was to switch identities, knock one or both of you out and then . . . seal the deal. Actually, that's genius."

Storme stood up, thought a minute, and sat back down again fast. "But to do that to Craig. The ethics of it. Drug Craig?"

Marsha chuckled. "Consent is a fact here. We can't deny that."

Storme screeched. "And drug me?"

Marsha nodded. "Do you really want to know Craig and Sunny made your baby together?"

Storme put her hands over her ears. "La-la-la. Can't hear you. Of course not! You didn't give her anything, did you?"

Marsha shifted in her seat. "Well, I am her mother. I did give her something . . ."

Storme screamed. "What? Mother! How could you?""

"Relax. It was a piece of my mind. There are such . . . recipes . . . but give her anything? Yes. I did."

Storme reared up. "What?"

"I gave her advice."

Storme made a gimme gesture. "And that was . . ."

"To talk to you. And I'll tell you something as well."

Storme cocked a brow and turned toward her mother, listening hard.

"You talk to Sunny. Talk to Craig. Talk to Jesse. Be careful of things done in secret."

On a dime, Storme turned from her mother and strode into the shop to retrieve her packages. Then she stormed away, heading for Samson, her car. *Easier said than done. Talking to Craig and Jesse is going to be tough. What do I say? But realistically,* do *I want to know if Sunny and Craig were to . . . to make a baby for me? Do I want a baby that bad? A knock-out drug for Craig? A Twin Switch? Seriously?*

Chapter Four: Do You Want to Know A Secret?

Storme jumped into her Samson and drove like a stream of speeding bullets out of an AR15 to Sunny's cabin. She didn't bother knocking. She didn't see Jesse's car in the lot, but Sunny's was there. *Good. She's home.*

She charged inside. "Sunny Ann Days! Where the hell are you?"

Sunny's voice came from afar. "In the can, if you must know. Geesh. What's your problem?"

Storme stood in the bathroom doorway and tapped her foot with impatience. "You! You. Are. My. Problem."

Stunned, Sunny bleated. "Moi? What'd I do?"

"You talked to Mom and made a decision I haven't agreed to. You decided to become my surrogate!"

"You're welcome. That was sisterly of me. Besides, you suggested it, not me."

Storme drew herself up to her full five feet three inches, making herself as big as possible. She glared at Sunny as if she were crazy while she finished her business. "We did not discuss this. We haven't gone through our list yet. We're still conducting research. Have you forgotten your kissing Craig nearly broke me and almost eighty-sixed our relationship?" She was dumbstruck by Sunny's reaction.

She literally could not catch her breath, let alone speak. After struggling with her self-control and her strained vocal cords, she screeched, "What I said was a mistake, a brainstorming screw-up. Why didn't I think of that? Oh yeah, now I remember. You tried to seduce my husband once upon a time in the recent past. A part of my soul *died* that day. A piece I'll never get back. It was soul murder, Sunny." Tears filled her eyes and were mirrored in Sunny's.

In that instant, an entire catalog of flashbacks raced through Storme's mind in living color. Sunny stealing her clothes and shoes, Abe, taking her place for Prom. Sunny eating her snacks, pretending she wasn't the guilty one. Craig copping a feel, and Sunny returning his kiss . . . One thought after another thumped through her mind like wet clothes in the dryer.

"It was a case of mistaken identity," Sunny said. "He thought I was *you*. I didn't seduce him. So shoot me. Don't use my help." She spun on her heel and made to leave. "I feel awful about what happened with Craig. It's hard to forgive myself for it. I didn't even realize I stole a piece of your heart. Lord, I feel just terrible about it." She raised her hand in a Girl Scout salute. "I really do. Scout's honor."

Storme put her hands over her heart. "Not just my heart, Sunny. It went way deeper into my very soul."

Sunny raced to her and hugged her long and hard, a hug that begged understanding and forgiveness. "I have to wrap my head around this. Think of it through your eyes and not just my own. I didn't intend to *wound* you. I wasn't thinking. I was screwing around, taking advantage of Craig, and stealing a momentary thrill. It was a heartless, thoughtless mistake. I am so *ashamed* of myself."

Storme shook her head and turned on her heel to leave. "That's the problem—right there in a nutshell. You never think first. But your antics have consequences, and this is a big deal."

Sunny chased after her, looking as if she had sucked on a

lemon. "Don't go charging away. You can't run from the truth or the past, and neither can I. I am *trying* here. That was then, this is now. Give me a chance to grow up. You've obviously been suffering for some time, while I've been hoping and praying I was past that sort of behavior. What I did is hard to own. I go in and out of denial. You know the drill. You know me. Old habits are hard to break. I was thinking outside of the box. But this time, I wanted to help, not hurt you. The Twin Switch had real potential and still does. I'm sorry." She paused for a moment, then added, "Brainstorming here. We either dope Craig, get him drunk, or . . ." She snapped her fingers. "I got it. You jack him off . . . and at the last moment, I climb aboard and viola, one baby coming up. That'll show you how sorry I am. I'd do *anything* for you – even give birth."

Storme swallowed the hard lump in her throat and fought against the knot of anxiety in her gut. The time of blame and shame was over. She and Sunny were grown women despite the ideas they were currently planning. One more wild, stupid thing, then motherhood would be within her grasp. She pushed her vanity and developing adulting aside and made her pride take its final dive.

Sunny actually sounded sincere about trying to help. "No, I get it. I really do. What I did was terrible. There's no excuse, and I'm still trying to make that up to you. Why else would I consider carrying your baby? We kinda already automatically culled our brainstorming list. You're on your way to baby-making." She started ticking things off the list. "You said you were getting the herbs and whatnot from Mom. I know because she gave me the same stuff so I can help conceive. You decided IVF and adoption were too expensive, and all the tests were too invasive. You hate needles, so acupuncture is out and costs time and money. The only thing left is to use my DNA, which is also yours, and Craig's sperm. I recommend surrogacy cuz there's nothing else on the list! We just have to convince you, Craig, and Jesse. You're just mad because I marked things off the list and got to the conclusion faster than you did. Not bad for a scatterbrain if I do say so myself."

"Fuck a duck, you're right. But I still hate the whole thing."

Sunny nodded, a smug grin tugged the corner of her mouth. "I know."

"Mom said she had . . . recipes . . ."

Sunny made a face. "Those are mighty potent. Remember Jesse and the love potion?"

"I'll say! Who you gonna drug anyway?"

"I'm not sure yet. Maybe Jesse and me? I just wanted to get our ducks in a row, ya know? We'll need a couple of spells or potions or whatever Mom does. Ones for conception—"

"More like deception, you mean," Storme groused.

Sunny grimaced. "Call it what you will. A potion for cooperation, compassion . . ." A gleam appeared in Sunny's gaze. "And maybe even passion."

Storme was beginning to see why and where Sunny's thinking was leading. "So, you'd carry my—our—Craig's . . . Geesh, whose baby is it anyway?"

"Yours. My identical egg. Craig's sperm."

Storme was getting on board now. "Do we just ask the guys? Convince them?"

"Whatever it takes. Shake on it."

Storme bit her lip but shook Sunny's hand. "We're in this together." She added, "We have to at least get informed consent, shouldn't we?"

"You've been hanging out with a lawyer too much."

"Who is the *Father* after all, but I actually got that from Dawn. And if you want to know the truth . . . Mom."

"I didn't know you had talked with Dawn."

"I texted Dawn and talked to Mom. Dawn sent me a lot of links to follow. They were all too overwhelming—lotsa gobbledygook about checking ovaries and fallopian tubes, my uterus. But I got her input. I can't do as she suggests. We don't have health insurance, hence Mom and Dr. Cyd's homeopathic practices."

"Operation Baby is in full gear. First step . . . talk to the men."

Storme shook her head. "No, first step is we all try the shakes, track periods, and ovulation while Craig and I make love. Second step remains to be seen. Truth or trick? But you do have to talk to Jesse. He has to agree that it's okay for you to become a surrogate."

Sunny nodded. "Makes sense."

Storme pinched her fingers. "We do have a teensy, little bitty problem, though. From the research we've done, and from what Dawn said, you don't qualify for surrogacy."

"Say what?"

Storme gulped. "Doctors want a candidate who has given birth *prior* so they know she can conceive and carry a baby. Plus, another surrogate is costly. You come cheap. Wanna be Godmother and surrogate?"

Sunny grinned, then grew serious. "Yup."

Storme bowed her head and cleared her throat. "Thanks, Sunny. I mean it."

They pulled up the calendar on her computer and started counting and tracking.

Storme added. "I bought an ovulation kit this afternoon."

"Good, that'll help."

Then Sunny paused, "Hang on, Storme, how long are you going to track things? It's mid-summer. Time's running out."

"Hmm . . . I was thinking maybe through October. If nothing happens by then, we get the men—actively—involved in this plan."

Storme could practically see the wheels turning in Sunny's head.

Sunny finally nodded. "Yeah, by December, I'll be pregnant by hook or by crook."

"Or turkey baster!" Storme reminded.

Sunny smiled. "Don't forget about Ghost Stag. I hope my pregnancy with your baby counts toward that."

"Me too. But we do things together. Remember the mumps?"

Sunny puffed out her cheeks. Her face looked like a blowfish. "That was *so* not fun."

"I know. Tell me about it. Chickenpox sucked, too."

Sunny squeezed her fingers together until a little space showed through. "We have only one other teensy-weensy problem . . ."

"Oh, what's that?"

"Neither of us have has regular periods. Never have."

"Too true. Here's what we do. We all, men too, take the herbs, shakes, teas, and do the sleep thing. Who knows, maybe I'll end up pregnant, and you will too. If by October nuthin' happens, we'll involve the men directly."

"How so?"

"We discuss surrogacy."

"Okeydokey. But not the Twin Switch thingy?"

Storme held back her grimace. "When—or *if*—we have to. I still need to think about doing the Twin Switch. It's more complicated than taking an exam for the other or switching name cards on a chicken dinner. Just saying"

"Good point, but let's keep it on a need-to-know basis for now."

Chapter Five: Trying to Have My Baby

Over the next several weeks, Storme continued eating right and checking her fluids. Dr. Cyd encouraged her to try meditation and gave her several tapes designed to help the process, which involved several facets.

Taking deep breaths in and out, counting them, and focusing on her breathing was okay. She could do that. But when she tried to clear her mind, she either thought of everything under the sun or fell asleep. Other times her head felt like it was full of cotton or static. She thanked heaven that baby-making kept her attention, concentrating her thoughts, if not clearing them. *Meditation is just not for me. It makes me mad at myself for getting distracted. I miss me when I'm not myself.*

At least I can visualize a baby snug and warm tucked in under my heart. Sometimes, meditation makes me horny. I keep picturing us doing it doggie style . . . Even missionary style. Not making love every day is a pain, but sex between us is never boring.

One afternoon in September, Storme entered Mellow Magic Apothecary to stock up on rose jam and raspberry tea. Both were part of the natural ways to boost fertility and support ovulation. Her mother and Dr. Cyd were chatting behind the counter.

"Hi, Storme, how goes it?" Cyd greeted.

Storme frowned. "So far, not so hot. I'm restocking my *get pg* supplies, hoping against hope I don't start my period again."

Cyd picked up a ginger root and five garlic cloves. "You'll need these. Grind the ginger for nausea when the time comes and chew on these cloves in the meantime."

"No, thank you."

Cyd just looked at her as if she had pronounced the sky pink.

"Chew garlic? I want Craig to make love to me, not run for the hills to get away from my dragon mouth."

Cyd chuckled and put them down. "Keep me in the loop during this process."

"Believe you me, I will. For sure."

The autumn leaves were frosting some hardwoods with shades of yellow, red, and orange, and the evergreens broke through for contrast. She felt blessed, not only for the awesome, breathtaking mountain view but for her overall good fortune. The breeze whispered *yeeesss* as if conferring its mountain blessing.

When the end of September rolled around, she was close to desperate and almost ready to try anything—including pulling off a Twin Switch. But before she told Sunny, she knew she and Craig had to talk.

But Storme was not chuckling later that afternoon when gripping menstrual cramps forced her to her bed. She knew she'd be flowing by suppertime. *Good thing I have a simple hotdog and corn on the cob dinner planned.* She grabbed her trusty hot pad and went fetal in their bed. She pulled the covers over her head and shut the world out. Grief for all her hopes and fears of motherhood once again had her in heaving, deep sobs.

She felt the warmth of Holly curling up beside her to comfort her and sighed. *So many poor, unfortunate single young women and girls find themselves in unplanned pregnancies. Yet here I am, ready and fortunate,* wanting *a baby, but so far, it's been nine months of nothing.* She'd had a period in August and now one in September. Time was running out. She was desperate.

Storme felt her control skid like a car on black ice during a freezing drizzle. Her tears just would not stop. Sometimes her grief short-circuited her brain and her judgment. *Why else would I even consider setting Sunny up to sleep with Craig*?

When Craig got home, he was dead tired. Storme wasn't on the deck to greet him. Even Holly seemed subdued and couldn't be found. Usually, she was winding herself around his legs, competing with his wife for attention. He found Holly, tail twitching, licking Storme's face. He knew it was tear-covered from the way Holly was behaving. She was really a honey of a cat, reading her peeps accurately each and every time. He realized Storme's period had come again.

He approached her bedside quietly, gently nudging Holly out of the way as he planted butterfly kisses where the tears had stained her face. "Period came, eh? Aww, babe."

Storme pulled herself up into his arms and let her misery pour out of her. All her broken hopes and dreams were displayed in shards of tears and pain around her eyes. "I've done everything they have told me to do, and still no baby." Holly's plaintive meow seemed to echo her words.

Real regret creased Craig's face. "I know. I have too."

Storme got out of bed and detached herself from him, hugging herself as if she were cold. "Maybe we should do the basal temperature thing?"

Craig got up and followed her from their bedroom to the Great Room. He sat in an armchair while she and Holly curled themselves into the corner of the couch. "I think we're trying too hard. I hate to think how crazy it could get with charts and thermometers. We have a good thing that just seems to happen between us. I hate to be ruled by a degree on a basal thermometer and numbers on a calendar. We've been using the diet and shakes only a couple of months. I've seen those chick flicks about wives tackling their men just to get pregnant. I like how we do things. I hate for us to get all technical and mechanical. We have such a great sex life. Never a chore. Baby-making can become just that—work. Let's not take the fun out. We're still newlyweds." He tweaked her breast, copping a feel. "Can we agree to give it another month before we figure out the next step?"

She nodded. "Should I try Clomid?"

"What's that?"

"A fertility hormone or drug. Makes you ovulate and release eggs."

"Let's wait on that. I've heard other men say messing with hormones can make your moods swing, making people crazed and crazy with the whole thing. As it is now, we have enough to worry about. COVID-19 is getting worse, money is tight. Give Mother Nature a chance."

The next day, Storme drove into work and helped Skye with some Lodge business. Eve, their oldest half-sister, was there too. She had been COVID-19-free since the summer. They met in the Lodge's office despite Storme's worry about the virus. The sisters and their families really did take the CDC's regulations seriously. With two members recently recovered from coronavirus, how could they not? They kept their visits within the ten-person limit and met outside whenever possible. Currently, no one occupied their field hospital at the Lodge, but there were fears the second wave of COVID-19 would hit in the fall.

Skye, Storme, and Eve reviewed the bookkeeping. It took them well over an hour to understand the system. Before Skye left, she motioned for Storme to join her beside the river rock fireplace off to the side where there was a cozy nook. They had privacy there.

Very few tourists were at the Lodge due to the barracks and field hospital, but the Park itself was packed with tourists. COVID-19 guests, as the family called them, were temporary residents. This included Eve and her fiancé, Beau. Dawn, Eve's twin, was there, too—on assignment with the National Guard—along with her intended, Drew.

Skye came into the nook carrying a diaper. When she sat, she asked, "Remember when I was in Scotland and learned I was pregnant?"

Storme nodded, wondering where this conversation was going, and looked at the cloth in Skye's hand. "Uh, pardon me, but why do you have a diaper and no baby in sight? Are you going to dust?"

Skye giggled. "Moi, dust? With quadruplets at home—hardly. At the doctor's office in Scotland, some grannies were there, discussing ways of conceiving in the old days. Seems one of their daughters was having trouble conceiving, so one old gal pulls out a cloth diaper and says, *Give 'er this. Slip it under the mattress and then make love. They'll be a bun in the oven in no time, provided two generations of women laugh and cry over this diaper. This is from my Fiona's wee one. It's hot. Her baby is eleven months, and she thinks she's expecting again.*" Skye crossed her heart. "True story."

Storme laughed.

"Fine, be that way. I'm trying to help, here."

Storme stopped laughing. "You're as bad as Sunny and her turkey baster method. Wait, is that how you conceived the kids?"

"No! My pregnancy was a complete shock! Having a baby was sooo far from my mind. I had no idea and wasn't even thinking about babies. What do you have to lose? Try it. What if it works?"

Storme and Skye were still laughing when Marsha and Eve joined them. Storme repeated the story, and they all laughed until they cried. Each took turns wiping their eyes on different sections of the *hot* diaper and then started laughing again.

Storme sat up. "OMG! Three generations of women – us – just laughed and cried over Skye's baby diaper. I'm trying this as soon as my period ends."

Marsha said, "I've been reading Dr. Hildegard von Bingen, and she used the four elements to work with the human body. We're all praying, too. You're eating produce from the earth, using water, from your energy and Craig's there's fire's life force . . . kundalini, and all that." She raised her finger to her head in apparent thought. "Hmm, have Craig stop by the shop. I've thought of something. Gotta go. Bye"

As soon as she left, Storme carefully tucked Skye's *hot* diaper in the inside pocket of her fleece, hoping to add her own mojo to the mix.

She texted Craig to stop at Mellow Magic Apothecary.

Craig chuckled. He had just finished stopping at St. Mary's religious article counter and found a Saint Gerard medal on a chain. St. Gerard was the Patron Saint of Mothers. *What harm could checking in with Marsha do?*

The trip to Marsha's shop would take mere minutes. Her shop was practically across the street. When he entered the store, she was lighting a candle. Although he could not identify the scent, it smelled great. Not for the first time, he wondered if it contained cannabis. He pushed the thought of legalities out of his mind. *Not my circus. Not my monkeys.*

"There you are! So glad you're here. My order for crystals and stones just came in." She handed him several stones and pointed to some crystals. She led him to the counter behind the register. "This pendant contains a carnelian and moonstone. Both are good for fertility. Moonstone has female energy. Makes sense, doesn't it, since the menstrual cycle is intricately connected with the lunar cycle?"

She lifted a pair of orange stone cufflinks. "These are for you. They contain carnelian and rose quartz set inside pyrite. That's a powerful combo for men."

She removed her earrings. "My Cherokee grandmother gave me these Apache Tears. Our ancestors can intervene if she wears them day and night." She piled several vials containing bath oils and salts.

"Whoa, Nelly! We'll have a baseball team with all this stuff."

Marsha chuckled. "Clomid will do that, not these elements."

Craig drew a hand across his forehead. "Phew. I'm not up for that anyway. Too forced and contrived."

"I hear you. These are natural, of the earth, not hormonally based. All these do is draw peace, health, and fertility. If Storme wants to become a mother—moonstone, the stone of new beginnings, is one of your best chances. It aligns with the moon's feminine energy, representing emotional stability and tenderness, balancing her cycles, her own hormones, and metabolism. Moonstone controls menstrual cycles, reduces stress, and encourages conception. Make love on a full moon while placing the stones under the pillows. And after that, have her wear the necklace."

"You really think there's something to this?"

She nodded. "The shamans of my people and many Chinese folks do too. If that's not enough, go next door and tap on Dr. Cyd Garden's door. Did you know I have a degree in Pharmacology?"

Craig was dumbfounded. "I guess I never knew that."

"Never judge an old hippie. We studied things. The whole Back to the Earth movement? That was us. I went to Berea College and around the world, honing my skills. Even learned from the Seminoles in Arizona."

"I had no idea!" A huge yawn overtook him.

"Figures. The girls know me for my maternal malpractice, not my homeopathy. No harm done."

The bell on Marsha's door jingled. "Speak of the Devil."

Cyd, similarly clad to Marsha, walked inside. "Hey, everybody."

"We were just talking about you," Marsha said.

Cyd winked. "Ah, so that's why my ears were ringing!"

Marsha chuckled. "No, that was the bell from the door."

Cyd smiled, too. "Now I know where Storme gets her wicked sense of humor. Hey, Craig."

Craig smiled a greeting and yawned again.

Ever on the alert for people's health, Dr. Cyd asked, "Is Storme wearing you out with all that baby-making?"

"No. This has gone on quite a while before that. I just can't sleep. Tried all the natural stuff. Still not sleeping."

Cyd peered over her glasses. She removed a prescription pad from her pocket. "Time for the big guns, then." She scribbled the scrip, ripped off the sheet, and looked him in the eye. "This a powerful and potent drug. Take as advised. There are some serious side effects. Whatever you do, keep me in the loop—just to be on the safe side."

He grimaced. "Like what?"

"Sleep-walking and eating."

"Sleep eating? That's a thing?"

"It's a real possibility. So is memory loss, holes in your recall, and increased sexual behavior. Let me know—immediately—if you experience any of that."

Craig's hands shook as he took the piece of paper. "I hate to resort to that, but nothing else has worked. What'd you prescribe?"

"Ambien. Just a week's worth." Cyd nodded. "You can't continue on like this. It's not healthy. You need rest."

Marsha gathered items, placing them carefully in boxes and hemp bags. "I was telling Craig here about the power of stones and crystals, but I think he's a doubting Thomas. I just told him to go talk to you, but here you are right on cue."

Once again, Cyd peered over her electric blue half-glasses matching her electric blue hair. "She's probably right about her assessment. When crystals are held close to the body, the human electromagnetic field changes. While healing occurs, crystals absorb the body's negative energies and release positive energy that the body absorbs, producing energy-level equilibrium. I see you have fertility crystals. You both should use them."

Marsha looked at Craig directly. "Wear your cufflinks."

Craig raised his shirtsleeves. "Done."

Marsha beamed.

Cyd gave a fist pump. "My man! Crystals used for conception have their own frequency, dependent on the element arrangement within their chemical composition. Every element vibrates at a particular frequency, and subtle healing energy is released by this vibration. The energies emitted by crystals rely on the special way their components vibrate in the inner crystalline structure. So if you're using crystals, they'll function to regulate sperm motility and fertility in both parents."

Craig removed his wallet from his pocket. "Then I'm set. I'll get these to Storme right away. Thanks." He tried to pay.

Marsha refused the money and winked. "I'll take it out of my babysitting bill."

He looked over his shoulder as he left. "I picked up a Saint Gerard medal for Storme."

Marsha beamed. Her smiled creased her face, and the fan lines at her eyes creased. "Then we covered all the bases. No stone left unturned. Good luck."

Craig left with a spring and an extra pep to his step.

Chapter Six: The Charms

When Craig got home, he found Storme asleep on the couch. She must have heard Holly's hello meow, because she woke up.

She rubbed her eyes. "Geesh, so much for meditating. I fall asleep . . . Every. Single. Time." A yawn interrupted her. "Hmm, what have you got there?"

Craig laughed, ruffled her hair as he planted a kiss on her lip, and sat on the floor beside her. He stretched out his arms to display his cufflinks.

"Pretty snazzy there, fella. Where'd ya get 'em?"

He grinned. "Ya think? I saw your Mom and Cyd, remember? She gave me fertility cufflinks. These stones are supposed to help my swimmers, uh, swim, I guess."

Storme ruffled his hair. "Aww. You're sexy when you come home in fertility charms."

He laughed. "You wait. There are some goodies for you, too."

She cocked a brow. "Do tell."

He withdrew the moonstone and carnelian pendant. "Wearing this will get your female parts balanced or charged up or sumthin' like that." Lifting her long locks, he kissed the back of her neck while he fastened the necklace around her throat. "Wear this after we make love when the moon is full, too."

She grabbed at the purple Mellow Magic bag. "You have tons of stuff. What is all this?"

"You name it. We have it."

Storme sneaked a peak. "Wow, looks like incense, crystals, candles, bath salts, oils . . . You got that right, everything but the proverbial kitchen sink."

He chuckled. "You're sure that's not in there too?"

She smiled as she continued to rummage through the purple bag. Some packets held small cards attached to the ties. "This says place this sachet of crystals on my ovaries during meditation. Fat chance. They'll probably help me nap or make a grocery list at the rate my meditation sessions are going."

She got up, kissed him, crossed the room to the far side kitchen section of their open concept house, and began ladling out fennel and cabbage vegetable soup. She paired it with a huge fresh leafy green salad and warm crusty bread. "Why don't you put a fire on? Ambiance and all that, we'll eat fireside."

"Oh wait!" He withdrew the earrings from his suit jacket pocket. "Wear these. They're Apache Tears from your mother . . ."

She laughed. "Meant to achieve maximum fertility, right, invoke our Cherokee and Apache ancestors?"

He joined her, kissing the top of her black hair as she titled her head to push the earring through her ear. "That's not all."

Her voice squeaked. "There's more?"

"I stopped by St. Mary's and got you this. It's a St. Gerard medal. He's Patron Saint of Mothers."

She hugged him and kissed him soundly before placing her hands over her heart. "Thanks for getting on board"—she waved her hands around—"with all this hoopla."

He winked. "Know what I'd like to get on board? You."

Her tone of voice held a little doubt and a whole lotta fear. She picked at her sweater, betraying her anxiety. "You think I'll *really* become a mother?"

"I do."

A week later, Storme's period was finally over, and the moon was full. Craig lay waiting in their bed as Storme lit a stick of incense from Marsha's goody bag. He smiled as she added a prayer for a sweet little baby of their own.

Craig immediately launched into a coughing fit when the smell of the incense reached him. "I think that must be a COVID-19 stick, the way it makes me cough. Get it outta here."

Storme doused it, causing more smoke and more coughing. The mood dampened. His plan for lovemaking was replaced by pounding on his back and applying *Vicks VapoRub* to his chest. Which didn't help with the mood or the cough. It wasn't exactly an aphrodisiac.

The next morning, he leaned over Storme for some make-up nooky, sneaking his hand between her thighs. "Let's make a mini-Storme."

She sighed as he traced his turgid rod over the route his hands had made to her hot center.

"Be careful there, big guy," Storme murmured. "We could be making a mini-Sunny."

Craig froze, and his cock deflated, and that ended that. He wasn't sure how to respond to Storme's comment. He reached out to her, but not before she took exception to his reaction, gave him the cold shoulder, and rolled away. From the set of her body, Craig knew his chances to get lucky—or answers—were not happening.

Storme couldn't believe she'd slipped up with her *mini-Sunny* comment. Luckily, Craig didn't say anything about it. She resolved to keep quiet next time.

When the next time came, Storme bathed in the fertility bath salts and applied lavender oil to her skin. She used rose-scented body powder—just in case he needed extra incentive . . . According to her mom, all these were guaranteed to aid in baby-making. It was way better than the pungent odor of the vapor rub.

Only one problem . . . Craig had a sneezing fit.

Rats! Foiled again. That session was spoiled. Who knew he was sensitive to so many scents?

Storme called Sunny the next morning.

Once Sunny stopped laughing, she counseled, "Just do it. Forget the trimmings. Every time you added something to the mix, you invite a jinx. Remember the hot sauce you massaged Craig with last winter? Haven't you learned anything?"

"I got that from Mom. It was called *Heavenly Hot.*" Storme chuckled. "You should have seen him hop all over the place before he doused his rod under the bathtub's cold-water faucet."

Sunny repeated. "Just hop to it. You should be careful when using Mom's stuff. Just saying. Oh, I meant to tell you, the Mosie Fertility Kit came."

"Now, you sound a lot like Mom!"

Sunny huffed. "Doesn't hurt to have a back-up plan. Beats a Twin Switch idea."

Storme didn't smile. "We may have to start taking that one seriously . . ."

"For reals?"

"For real."

Sunny's voice rose. "Yowzer!"

Later on, in desperation, Storme tucked Skye's diaper gift beneath the mattress cover on her side of the bed. That night, after watching *The Bachelor* together on television, she simply showered and used her usual shampoo. No oils, no salts, no bath powder, just her and her own pheromones. Nor did she light candles, wear perfume, or jewelry. *Naked ole me will just have to do.*

As they whispered sweet nothings to each other, Craig made a special request. "We didn't go overboard with charts and ovulation cycles or temperatures like I worried about, but we have used jewelry, medals, scents, rocks, and crystals. Can't we just make love in peace?"

Storme nodded, deciding not to focus on the old wives' tale and Skye's tyke's diaper, and gladly agreed.

She liked nothing between them but skin. She loved this man with her whole self and set out to prove it. As her hands ran over his strong arms, she felt his muscles quiver when he held her tight. Arms that felt so right . . . were so right. Arms that protected her and kept her safe. Arms that held power and love.

She ran her fingers across his ripped, broad, sexy chest and kissed his nipples until they hardened. With each love bite she nibbled, her body sang the same song his responsive body did. She felt his rod stiffen and lowered her hands to sift through the springy hairs that coved the space above his cock. She went lower to the base of his balls and let her fingers flick over them. Then she guided him into her warm, ready folds.

Chapter Seven: Love Potion Number Nine

Storme decided it was time to talk to Sunny again. *We gotta get a real plan.* She texted her twin.

U up 4 a walk? Gatlinburg Trail.

In return, she received a *thumbs-up icon. Time?*

1 hour?

K

The sky was the perfect shade of bright beautiful blue with an occasional puffy white cloud providing contrast to the amazing blue expanse. The colors of the trees were breathtaking, ablaze with red, yellow, and orange hues. God's artistry drew the tourists and locals alike into the Park. The forest scents of cedar, pine, and hickory laced air, and the temperature was in the 60s. Storme didn't even need the fleece top she had on. She wore skinny black jeans and stylish running shoes—despite not being a runner. Her aviator shades completed her look.

Sunny, wearing a nearly identical outfit, smiled in greeting. "What's up?"

"Operation Baby needs help. I'm not pregnant."

Sunny shrugged. "Neither am I."

Storme glared at her twin. "You better not be! That'd leave us with few options."

Sunny nodded. "There's the good ole turkey baster. That's better than slipping Craig a Molly, which is supposed to have memory loss associated with it. Plus, the Twin Switch should be our *last* resort. *If* we do a Twin Switch . . . hate to say that—

"

"I hate that idea," Storme growled. "I should never have suggested it in the first place."

Sunny nodded. "But desperate times call for desperate measures. Just sayin'."

"Extasy could be difficult to get. I've heard it's dangerous. He could overdose and die. It's probably against the law and involves no consent. Not goin' there."

Sunny's lips formed a grim line, and she shook a finger at her. "You've got marital bed consent already."

"That isn't even a thing."

"Is too."

"Is not. The law says sex must *always* be consensual."

"Duh, the marriage thing?"

Storme paused to think. "I guess if I initiate and he reciprocates . . ."

" . . . and I slip in . . . and you slip out . . . it sorta counts. Right?"

Storme bit her lower lip. "I dunno. Don't think so."

"What's the diff between Mom slippin' a love potion in Jesse's sweet tea and a Mickey for Craig?"

"The love potion was probably unethical and illegal, too!"

Sunny snapped her fingers. "I know. Let's get him skunk drunk. Hmm, let's all get drunk, so we can carry this off and not chicken out."

"I don't think so . . . alcohol messes with fertility."

Sunny puffed the curls off her brow as she walked. "Then what's the point of all this? Give him one of those Ambien Dr. Cyd prescribed. Doesn't he have trouble sleeping? That makes people do stuff they don't even know about, and he won't know it's me, not you. We hafta get serious here. Jesse is going to be out of town this Wednesday, and I can stay with you two. Get ya drunk, do the switch and the deed, and viola, a baby is made. Now's our chance."

Storme was too aggravated. Her conscience was waging a war that felt every bit as fierce as the Civil War. "You'll have to talk to Jesse first."

"He'll never agree to a Twin Switch."

"No, but he might accept a surrogacy. We at least need *his* consent. Otherwise, he'll think the baby is his."

"Oh yeah. Duh. Okay, I'll talk to him about that."

The trail led them to the bridge over the Little River. Storme looked down and spotted a nice-sized brown Brook Trout. Its tail caught the sunlight when it leapt to catch an insect. The wind whistled through the leaves. *Trrryyy* . . .

Storme took that as a sign that they were on the right track.

They turned around and headed back to the trailhead. Storme and Sunny seldom finished the rest of the trail to the Sugarlands Welcome Center. The tree cover had been cleared for outbuildings, and that section let the sun's rays shine harshly down on the path. It made the walk too hot for them.

Suddenly, Sunny stopped dead. "Tonight is Operation Consent for all of us."

Storme frowned. "Too bad we can't just tell Craig. Ask him for his semen . . ."

"And ruin all our fun? Schemes are part of our genetic make-up, and you just want to come out and tell him? Do you think he'll really jack off and let me what? Sit on his swimmers?"

Storme forced back the smile that tried to form on her face picturing that scenario. "No can do. After we nearly broke up over your kiss, how can I suggest that, let alone the rest of it? Not sitting but uh . . . uh . . . receiving shall we say . . . his sperm more directly? Besides, Craig said the kiss was a mix-up, mistaken identity, but this is a whole 'nother other. Messing with Craig's semen is serious stuff."

Sunny gave her last, best argument. "What makes you think he'll accept this whole other thing if he finds out?"

"I'm getting really lame and immature here. I'm hoping the baby's conception and birth will distract him. I'm planning on bringing up the surrogacy thing tonight, too. Operation Consent begins."

Chapter Eight: Making My Baby

After Storme left Sunny, she made an oyster casserole to accompany a kale and baby spinach salad with red ginger dressing. She planned to include honey date muffins, since they also assisted with conception. Indeed, the whole meal did. She had Craig's favorite pistachio pudding already made and waiting in the refrigerator. Finally, she threw together an onion and fennel soup to make sure the axiom *everything from soup to nuts* was covered for the meal. *All my bases dealt with.*

Once dinner was set, she took a shower and washed her hair with her usual coconut shampoo. She laughed as she recalled her research that claimed coconut was good for creating life and balancing hormones. She dressed in an off-the-shoulder blouse and leggings and slipped her bare feet into furry *UGG* boots.

As soon as Craig entered the door, he obviously caught a whiff of the oyster casserole and smiled. He loosened his tie, pulling it down, and rolled up his shirtsleeves, then washed his hands at the kitchen sink. The island was set for their dinner. The scent of dates and honey rose from the warm muffins already on the table.

"I'm sorry I'm so late for dinner. I hope I didn't cause any problems for you," Craig said.

Storme smiled. Her heart beat a fast staccato within her. How she loved this dude. "No problem. You texted before it was too late. I made you a dinner to remember."

A cocky grin covered his face. "Does it include a night to

remember, too?"

She winked saucily and sashayed over to him to kiss his luscious lips. "Ya never know."

He returned her kiss and slapped her on the ass. "It smells heavenly, you little tease."

"What, no sneezing or coughing at the aroma?"

He grinned. "Nope."

Storme pulled the bubbling oyster casserole from the oven and placed it on a trivet. She kept it warm with a lid. Then she ladled soup into their bowls. The salad was tossed, and the fresh dressing blended perfectly with the kale and baby spinach. Over dinner, she raised the topic. "It's October."

"Halloween isn't a good idea. Isn't it canceled due to COVID?"

"I'm not talking Halloween. I'm talking *baby*."

"That's scary!"

She buttered a muffin after carefully removing it from its accordion-pleated paper cup. "I'm not pregnant. It's time to think of other options."

"Okaaay . . ."

She paused and looked up at him. "I know our health coverage is lacking . . ."

He sighed. "More like barely there, you mean."

She nodded. "Adoption and IVF are not options."

He nodded. "Sadly."

She pressed on. "Adoption is expensive and not feasible under the circumstances. We don't want to do basal temps, and hormones and drugs are definitely out. And Mother Nature's been a bitch."

He looked at her with a trace of tears in his eyes. "There has to be an easier way . . ."

Her eyes welled up, too. "There is."

Hope filled both his eyes and tone. "There is?"

"Yup. Surrogacy."

His tone sharpened. "Surrogacy . . . Never thought of that . . ."

She chuckled. "Right?"

He raised his hand. "Hold on. That costs plenty, too. I dunno . . . How can that work? We can't afford one."

"I may be able to get someone. I'll look into it."

"Okay."

"Do you trust me?"

"Why wouldn't I?"

She giggled and pulled him by his tie into their bedroom. She undressed him, salting him with tender kisses, expressing how much she loved this man and everything about him. She kissed him with every ounce of her love and a heart full of gratitude, hope, and the deepest love she was capable of lavishing. She lay on her back and spread her legs wide in loving, joyful welcome. After he entered her, she drew her legs up and wrapped them around him, tilting her pelvis to take in as much of him as she could. She had no doubts concerning the depth of his love. They ground together so deeply she could feel his pubic hairs against her center, stroking her clit, increasing her pleasure and joy.

There was no doubt Craig was lost in sensations that were pure ecstasy. He sniffed her hair, and she felt him stiffen even more, if that was possible. She could tell how blown away he was by the low moans and groans issuing deep from within him. He was lost in her. There were no two ways about it. After a few more thrusts, he came apart, and she joined him spinning in the stratosphere.

Once her breathing calmed, she murmured softly, "My sister has my DNA. She could be our surrogate. Hey," she prodded him. "You listening?"

"Huh? Yeah. Whatever. She's stayin' with us. Okay?"

"Uh-huh."

Craig grunted and patted the space next to him. "Slide over

here. I want to fall asleep with you in my arms."

Storme slid into the warm cocoon he created just for them. He pulled Gram's quilt over them and spooned himself around her, snuggling into her heat.

CHAPTER NINE: WHY DELILAH?

Sunny helped Jesse pack for the few days he'd have to spend in Ashville, North Carolina. He needed to work with the Deltec design team concerning some renovations his clients wanted. She hated that he was leaving but was relieved she wouldn't be alone. She'd be staying with her sister Storme and her husband. Being alone spooked her. She knew she'd be safe and protected there at Storme and Craig's Mountain Magic home.

After dinner and a long lovemaking session, she could see the tension drain from Jesse's body and noticed he was feeling as mellow as she was. That was due in part to their afterglow and maybe, truth be told, the moonshine he'd consumed earlier.

Sunny found a cozy spot next to him and asked, "You asleep?"

His voice was thick, "Not quite."

"Storme can't conceive. Do you think I can?"

"Yup."

"Would you mind if I carried her baby?"

"Huh? Sure, why not?"

In the dark, Sunny's arm made a fist bump in triumph. "Just thinking is all. Good to know. G'night."

Loud snores were her response.

To be clear, the next morning Sunny said, "I'm so glad you're up for my becoming Storme's surrogate."

Jesse smiled. It was evident he was distracted. She could tell his attention wasn't fully on the conversation at hand.

When she launched into the details of a Mosie Kit, ovaries, and insemination process, he covered his ears. On a roll, Sunny continued to talk about ovaries, ovulation, speculum, specimen cup, fallopian tubes, uterus and the like.

Jesse screwed his face like he bit into a lemon. "TMI! I don't need to know all that female stuff. It's taboo. Stop talking. Puh-leeze."

Sunny smiled. It wasn't her job to understand. Jesse was responsible for what he heard or didn't hear. She couldn't understand it for him. His job was to pay attention to her and what she said.

Operation Consent? Mission accomplished. He said yes! Sunny reached for her phone to text the same to Storme. She added a *happy face emoji and a heart.* Then she typed her message.

Storme's phone pinged. She grabbed it to read its text.

Mission accomplished.

She returned a fist bump emoji, then cuddled closer to Craig. *Soon all my dreams will come true.* At that moment, her black and white dreams changed to glorious Technicolor. Both she and Craig slept in the following morning.

Wednesday afternoon, Sunny arrived at Mountain Magic with her duffle bag in hand. She was spending the next several days with Storme and Craig while Jesse drove to Asheville to work on his new project.

When she met up with Storme, they hugged each other—momentarily ignoring social distancing—giddy with joy.

"Spill," Storme blurted.

Sunny grinned. "You spill."

"I think I will." Storme launched into their dinner and the Knight's subsequent conversation. "I kinda slipped it in after we made love . . ."

Sunny approved. "Good thinking. That's always the best time to get anything. For eons, tons of women used sex as friendly fire when they went on the offense. Jesse's defenses were down as well. You say so were Craig's, but are you sure he heard you?"

Storme nodded. "Pretty sure. After all, I got your name, surrogacy, and *cheap* out."

"Close enough for government work."

Her twin chuckled and nodded. "I said my surrogate comes cheap."

Sunny slugged her. "Geesh. Some gratitude. Let me re-think this. Maybe I should charge you."

Storme rubbed her arm. "What are you, ten years old?"

The afternoon sun lit the trees as if they were on fire, blazing with oranges and reds, tinged with yellow leaves. Sunny and Storme chatted and plotted the afternoon away.

"Oh, I forgot," Sunny said. "I brought some hard cider for Craig. Tonight's the night, right? The Big Switch?"

"Yuppa. We're both ovulating according to the calendar and the test you just took. Remember, we gotta be nude, so he can't tell which is which. He's been taking Ambien lately, so go easy on the hard cider with him. Remember the plan."

"What's to remember? Get him high. Get on him, get him off, get off him."

"Yeah, just don't you get off on the sex. This is, uh"—Storme paused—"science, not fun."

Sunny stuck out her tongue. "Spoilsport."

Storme threw her twin a look that could kill.

Sunny made a cross with her fingers. "Kidding."

When Craig got home that night, he ordered a pizza from Ski Mountain Pizza and savored its delicious sauce and crust. Sunny made sure he ordered garlic butter breadsticks and cupcakes, too. It was a fast-food feast. They ate in front of a roaring fire in the fireplace while watching the flat-screen TV mounted above the mantelpiece. Neither Sunny nor Storme had the hard cider. They had regular non-alcoholic cider, but Craig could and did enjoy his.

Sunny laughed her way through *Jeopardy* as they all called out answers before the contestants. Later they watched the *Weakest Link*, then stayed up a little later than usual to cap the night off with Jimmy Kimble's monologue, and then went to bed.

Sunny wore short sleep shorts and a sleeveless t-shirt that belonged to Storme. She waited in Storme's walk-in closet, which was large enough to house a Victorian Ladies Fainting Couch that Storme used when she dressed.

Craig had his own walk-in and was not likely to enter Storme's. Sunny should be safe from his eyes, and he shouldn't get tipped off. Their plans were carefully constructed. So far, it was going like clockwork.

Sunny removed her PJs to be ready and lay on the couch. When she heard Storme starting to make love to Craig, she plugged her ears with shaking hands.

Storme had mentioned she planned to moan loudly when the time was right. Sunny strained her ears, listening hard, but nothing came of it. She couldn't hear a thing. Had Craig fallen asleep! *He must have taken an Ambien.*

Sunny, who might be a bit sleep drunk herself, was determined to wait for Storme's signal. But despite her good intentions, she felt her eyelids close and fell asleep.

A loud clap of thunder woke a still-naked Sunny in the wee hours of the morning. She fled the closet in terror to shakily climb into bed with Storme, cuddling in fear just as she had in childhood. Storme, long used to sleeping with Sunny, shifted to make room for her in the king-sized bed.

The shift in weight and vibrations in the bed woke Craig.

What the fuck! He opened his eyes to find two Stormes in his bed, and both were naked as blue jays! *I must be seeing double. Man, that Ambien shit is strong!*

He stumbled into the bathroom and grabbed a cold, cold glass of water, making sure he splashed lots of icy water on his face to clear his head. It didn't work, so he decided to get ready for work and took a frigid shower in hopes that would clear his brain.

Storme woke with a start when Craig got up and headed to the bathroom. Not so gently, she rolled Sunny out of their bed.

"Ouch," Sunny grumbled. "Be careful. You tryin' to kill me?"

Storme waved her hand. "Shh."

Sunny fled to the guest room and didn't surface again until after Craig left for his office.

"I couldn't do it!" Sunny cried as she entered the kitchen. "That was terrible. It went so horribly wrong. I'm so sorry."

Storme consoled her twin, patting her on the back as she hugged her hard. "You tried. I don't think I could either. Craig fell asleep, and so did I. I didn't wake up until he left the bed. We'll just hafta go the Mosie route."

Sunny whined, "But how we gonna get his sperm? Why can't he just . . . uh . . . you know . . . jack off and catch it in semen cup from the Mosie Kit?"

Storme considered it. "Hmm. Yeah. Why couldn't he? He can. He already agreed to let you carry the baby. You go home and get the kit."

Sunny looked down, but not before she flashed a cocky grin. "I brought the kit with me. To tell the God's truth, I was afraid of the whole Twin Switch thing. I didn't want to let you down, but I didn't know if I could, you know, actually *do* it."

Storme gave her a slight smile. "I know, sweetie. I had my

own doubts. Could I live with myself? Let you be so intimate with my man? It's okay. I get it. I really do." She hugged her sister again, feeling very moved. "We'll do this the right way. On the up and up. We'll use the Mosie Kit and cross our fingers."

"You'll have to help me insert it, or just be by my side as I do it. I don't want to mess up." She sighed. "There's a limit to how much I can take and how far I'll go. Who knew? Hey, I'm getting good at this adult thing."

Storme said, "We got this. Of course, I'll be there."

Sunny's face lifted. "Even though there's some deception in every relationship, I think I'll feel much better about this if the guys are on board and we're straight up honest. Well, as upfront as we get."

Storme laughed. "I agree. Text Jesse, and I'll talk to Craig. How about tonight? You're still ovulating."

"If we're all on board, I'm on board." Sunny snickered. "Or rather on Mosie!"

Chapter Ten: Tonight's the Night

When Jesse got Sunny's text, his jaw dropped. It read . . . *Come home pronto! I almost did something stupid. 2nite we make Storme a mom.*

He cut his trip short and immediately called Craig. "Do you know what the devil our twin wives are up to now?"

"Huh? Do I want to know?"

"Probably not."

The fog in Craig's head had cleared if nothing else. He rubbed a hand over his fatigued face, and his brow creased. He was sure he had some gray hairs now. After this. *What the devil are they up to this time?* The twins were well known for their capers and harebrained ideas and schemes.

When he spoke, his voice was shaky. "Uh. I'm not sure. There seems to be a hole in my memory. I can't remember a whole lot about stuff lately. It's a side effect of the Ambien I'm taking. Let me tell you, that is some serious shit. I feel like I don't know what I heard or what I think I heard, or what I saw or didn't see. I was actually seeing double last night. Two naked Stormes. I went to bed with one naked Storme and woke up with two!" He sighed deeply, pausing a second. "Lay it on me."

Jesse's voice was the one shaking now. "You . . . you don't think one of the Stormes was Sunny, do ya?"

Craig sat up ramrod straight, and his voice rose an octave. "Good God, no! How could that be?"

"Storme talk to you about surrogacy?"

"Um . . ." Craig hesitated before he spoke again. "Uh-huh. Something like that. I said we don't have the funds."

Jesse was slow to respond. He gulped, and there was a gasp in his hoarse response. "What else did she say?"

"Something about having an idea who might do it . . ."

"What if that someone was Sunny?" Jesse spoke in a rush.

Craig bolted upright, dropping his phone. He scrambled to find it and pick it up. "Hold on a minute. That's a wild supposition you're making. Son of a bitch."

"Sunny asked me if I minded whether she carried Storme's baby since neither she nor Storme was pregnant yet. I was thinking more of *holding* your kid, carrying it around in a sling thing those new moms use, not literally *carrying* a child inside her. I agreed to it."

"Stop. Just stop. Listen to yourself. That's crazy!"

"They're crazy."

Craig shook his head wildly, trying to think and hear straight. *I have a helluva hangover. Christ Almighty.* "You got something there." *No, it's the Ambien. It's messin' with my head. My wife wouldn't mess with anything like that, would she?*

"Sunny used a love potion on me . . ."

"Yeah, but you said you loved her and didn't need it."

"It didn't stop her, though, did it?"

Good Grief! "No. It did not. Meet me in my office." What was crossing his mind was inconceivable, wasn't it?

"See ya in a couple of hours."

"Drive safe."

"Will do. Bye."

Craig's thoughts tumbled like a litter of puppies, each one chasing the next and all spelling trouble. It was hard to think, harder still to make sense of what he did think. Snatches of their conversation came back to him. *Don't worry. Yes, you'll conceive. Yes, we'll try whatever it takes. Shakes, oysters, crystals. Shit! What did I agree to? Hormones? No, they'd passed on that.*

Didn't want to get crazy over this. Damn . . . Why did I ever take that Ambien? I did that, not Storme. Not Sunny.

The more he thought, the dizzier he got. Had one or both women slipped him a mickey? His thoughts collided and just didn't make sense. He held his head in his hands, wishing he could think straight or at least remember. He couldn't work, so he sent Mary Lou home. He paced his office, waiting—wanting and not wanting—to meet with Jesse.

The drive from Asheville took longer than Jesse wanted. The Smoky Mountain mist had rolled in and made the trip feel longer than it was and made him later than he expected. To top that, the full moon shone eerily through the mist. It was spooky . . . A perfect night for Halloween. Come to think of it, it was Halloween, and they were experiencing the second full moon of the month—a blue moon. As if his thoughts weren't frightening enough.

When he made it into Craig's Gatlinburg's law office, Craig opened his bottom desk drawer and removed a bottle of Scotch. He poured two fingers of it into the glasses he had nearby and offered one to Jesse.

"I think we're going to need this," Craig said.

Jesse nodded. "There's something planned for tonight. Sunny texted something about making Storme a mom to-night, and that means—"

"Oh lord! Sunny and Storme expect me to . . ."

"Dude! What the hell. I never meant Sunny could use you as a stud service." He laughed. "As if."

But Craig wasn't laughing. "It's not funny."

Chapter Eleven: Ain't No Sunshine

Sunny paced the floor. "The cat's outta the bag. All hell's gonna break loose. I kinda cleared things up with my text."

"What'd ya say?"

Sunny pulled the text up. "Read for yourself."

Storme looked. "That'll do it. The text is to the point and quite clear."

"How are we going to play this? They could be mad."

"Hold on. We got their consent."

"We go with that. We have to go on the offensive. What if we . . ."

They schemed for a while. But when Craig and Jesse walked in, it was crystal clear they were not happy campers.

This time there was no fancy dinner nor an aromatic dripping oozing cheese pizza. Sunny and Storme greeted their men with confidence and kisses, which did not throw the guys off their game.

Craig greeted Sunny with "Hello Ethel." Then he turned to Storme. "Lucy, you have some 'splaining to do."

This didn't seem like a time for batting the eyebrows, but Storme did deliver a perfect I Love Lucy *Wah*.

Sunny asked, "What do you mean, Craig?"

Craig frowned. "Don't give me that. Two naked Stormes in my bed?"

Storme huffed. "It's our bed. Is it my fault Ambien obviously made you hallucinate?"

Jesse nodded. "I've heard the side effects are a bitch . . ."

Craig looked shaken. "I find it hard to believe. You had a

fit when I kissed Sunny by mistake. Yet to think you'd deliberately—"

"Stop right there." Fury was in Storme's tone. "You gave consent. We discussed surrogacy."

"I didn't mean I'd sleep with Sunny."

Jesse barged into the conversation. "Hey, dude, close your mouth, or I'll—"

"You'll what?" Craig rounded on him. "Get charged with assault? This was your accusation, not mine. You floated that idea. Now I can't get it out of my head. Sunny, how could you?"

Sunny defended her position. "I agreed to be Storme's surrogate." She turned to Jesse. "What did you think? I was gonna sleep with him?"

Jesse looked taken aback.

"I said I'd carry her baby. Ya know, *bear* her baby. I can prove it. I have a Mosie—"

"If that's a new age mickey, no thanks," Craig grumbled.

Sunny ran to the guest room and came back with her Mosie Kit. "Get a gander of this." She threw it at Craig.

He fumbled the box. It fell, and the contents spilled out.

Sunny gathered the gloves, speculum, syringe, and semen cup. She removed the plastic wrap from the speculum and balled her fist. "This is how it works. My fist is my uterus and vulva."

Jesse's face paled as Sunny began to explain and demonstrate. "You simply take this speculum after Craig deposits his swimmers in this cup, and the mini turkey baster is filled. Place the speculum between my vulva . . ."

Jesse turned green and fainted.

Craig rushed to help Jesse to his feet while Storme got him a bottle of water.

Storme caught her attention and mouthed, "Good offense."

Sunny smirked at Jesse. "You wanted to know. Now you

do. I knew you didn't want too much female detail. Hmm, TMI, you said, and I quote, *Spare me the female stuff.*" She turned to address Craig. "There's an infomercial to watch, Craig, if you want more details."

Craig shook his head. "I need to think. I'll sleep at the office."

Worry strained Storme's voice. "What will folks—and Mary Lou, for God's sake—think?"

"I don't give a flippin' flamingo what she or anyone else thinks."

Storme battled on, iron in her tone. "I mentioned surrogacy and got your consent."

"A bit simplified, wouldn't you say? What an understatement," Craig grumbled.

"You said *Yes.* That's called informed consent, Mr. Lawyer. Jesse knew. Sunny knew."

Craig's face whitened. His voice dripped with ice, but fire blazed in his gaze. "Tell me, why did I see two naked women? Was one of them Sunny?"

Storme fumed. "How perverted do you think I am, buddy? Maybe you're the pervert for suggesting that. Sunny always sleeps nude."

Sunny smiled, and Jesse's nod confirmed her sleeping habit.

Storme's tone deepened. "She has always jumped into bed with me when there's a thunderstorm. She's afraid of storms."

Again, Jesse nodded that this was the case. "True."

Storme was on a roll. "Did *you* take any Ambien?"

Craig shifted, looking uncomfortable.

"Did you drink any hard cider?"

Craig squirmed.

"That's on you. Have you ever had nonconsensual sex?"

"You know I haven't—"

"Then don't blame my sister." Storme's voice rose an octave.

Sunny bolted upright and pointed at herself. "What? Blame, little ole moi?" She felt a little guilty for the way she and Storme were stretching the truth.

A dazed and confused expression crossed Jesse's face. "What just happened?"

Craig muttered in response. "Hell if I know."

Storme stamped her foot. "I rest my case."

Sunny popped up like a little prairie dog. "Not guilty."

Jesse made a suggestion. "Do me a favor, Craig. Call Dr. Cyd and see what Ambien does. Could be double vision or hallucinations are side effects. Just sayin', man."

Sunny jumped on that idea. "Can we start over?"

Craig headed for the door. "Maybe in the morning. Right now, I have to clear my head and think."

He stormed out.

CHAPTER TWELVE: WE SHALL OVER-COME

Sunny frowned as the front door slammed shut, then turned to Storme. "Looks like tonight's *not* the night. Should we leave?"

"No. Stay," Storme said. "Jesse, you're welcome to share Sunny's bed. That is if she'll let you within ten feet of her—without a ten-foot pole. What *exactly* were you thinkin'?"

Sunny echoed her twin's sentiments. "Yeah, what?"

Jesse sighed. "If it's all the same to you, do you mind if I stretch out on your couch? It's late and I'm beat. I'm sorry."

Sunny threw him a smile. "Come to Mama, baby."

Jesse went white.

"Poor choice of words." She crooked her finger. "Care to join me? I'm feeling forgiving."

"Think I'll shower, if y'all don't mind." Jesse trotted into the guest bathroom.

"Be my guest." Sunny smiled, then winked at Storme. "Well played. Told ya a good offense makes a good defense."

Jesse came out of the bathroom, shaking his head. "I don't care about the video. Maybe it's too much for me. But if these two decide to move forward, I say . . . Do it. Get it done. Move on."

"My hero."

The night was cloudy and cooler than usual for this time of

year. But then again, everything about 2020 was upside down, inside out, backward, and going sideways. What did Craig expect?

Somehow he found himself at Elkmont Cemetery. *Leave it to Storme to drive me to a cemetery, for God's sakes. Sometimes she drives me insane. But this one is too much. I know my wife . . . she could talk a statue into sitting down. I can't get over that the two of them would gaslight me despite their excuses. I know Storme wants a baby desperately, but . . . And that's a mighty big but.*

On autopilot now, Craig found himself at Emma Jean's grave. Emma Jean was Storme's Gram, but everyone had sought her out in life. Why should he be surprised now?

Emma Jean, what do I do? I wanna shoot Storme. How could she do this to me? To us? What was she thinking?

He bent down on his haunches and swept the downed leaves from around her tombstone. Suddenly, the clouds parted, and the blue October moon shone down, illuminating the words on her tomb. *Love one another as I have loved you.* Clarity rushed in just as the full moon lit up the night. When he heard the whisper of the trees, what he heard would stay with him forever. *Forgiiiive . . .*

He chuckled. *It's that simple. She loves me so much that she wants physical proof walking around. She needs Sunny to carry my baby? Fine. I can overcome my pride and cooperate. But if I have to watch that Posie – or whatever you call it – video, Jesse does, too. Hell, all four of us are in this now, so we should all watch it.*

He drove home and crawled into bed. Storme rolled on her side, and he spooned around her.

He let out a gentle sigh and whispered into her ear. "We'll overcome this. We'll talk in the morning."

Chapter Thirteen: Can't Stop the Feeling

Storme woke up and padded into the kitchen to start the coffee. Although she didn't feel like eating, she began *doin'-a-Gram,* cooking a good old-fashioned breakfast with all the trimmings. First, she turned on the ceiling fan—just in case she burned anything. Besides, cooking made her feel warm. She heard her grandmother's whisper in the light breeze that rippled across her cheek. *The way to a man's heart is through the stomach.*

She mixed pancake batter as the bacon and sausage fried. She even added eggs to the menu. Craig was the first to join her. As he embraced her from behind, his hands lightly, gently, and lovingly cupped her breast, and she turned in his arms to kiss his lips.

When the embrace and the kiss broke off, she whispered, "I'm sorry. "A lot of thinkin' and a good night's sleep helped me get it. You need a baby. You are obviously desperate to be a Mom . . . I can watch the *Posie* infomercial—"

"Mosie." She giggled and flipped a pancake.

"Huh?"

"It's called a Mosie. It can make me a baby, with your help, of course. Can't do it without you and your swimmers."

Jesse entered the kitchen sniffing, obviously having caught the bacon's aroma. "Do what? Or shouldn't I ask?"

Last to join them was Sunny. She tossed her bedhead locks, trying unsuccessfully to pat them into place, but the stubborn curly waves were not cooperating. "Coffee. I need coffee."

Jesse poured and handed Sunny a steaming mug of mountain-grown Joe.

After a few minutes, she perked up. "Is everything cool with everybody, or is it still all Hatfield and McCoys?"

Craig looked a bit sheepish. "No harm, no foul. I get it now."

Sunny dramatically drew her hand across her brow. "Phew."

Craig's cheeks flooded with color. "Let's all watch that video and see what we're in for."

Storme and Sunny high-fived each other, and Sunny pulled up the Mosie infomercial.

Storme almost laughed when the color leached from Jesse's face, but Craig seemed to be taking it in stride.

When the presentation was over, Jesse managed to say, "That was a whole lot less graphic than Sunny's rendition. You ovulating, Sunny?"

"Yep." She and Sunny answered in unison.

Jesse grimaced. "As I told Sunny . . . Do it. Get it done. Move on."

"Operation Baby . . ." Sunny crooned.

"Is on!" Storme added with gusto.

Craig snapped his fingers. "Hey, there's a full moon. Didn't the research say that's a good time to . . . uh . . . do this . . . this deed?"

"Right you are, baby." Storme hugged Craig with all the joy, love, and gratitude she had. "I'd like to roll in the hay right now, but we want your boys to be all primed and ready tonight."

Sunny giggled. "Talk about graphic. Craig's swimmers and my identical eggs will make a baby tonight when the moon is full."

Storme looked at Sunny. "Time to call Dr. Cyd. She said

she'd help us do this."

Sunny looked relieved. "Phew. I was kinda worried about that. I didn't want to screw it up."

"I know. That's why I have Dr. Cyd on call."

The four of them gathered in a circle, and Storme reached a hand to the center. Each of the others slapped a hand on top of hers like football players before a game.

Storme nodded at Sunny and Jesse, then smiled at Craig. "We got this."

The full moon shone brightly through the windows as Storme followed Craig into their bedroom.

"Talk about awkward . . ." Craig murmured.

"It doesn't have to be. I can give you a hand job and viola."

He grinned. "Rather have a blow job."

"Sorry. Can't contaminate the specimen."

They stripped and kissed and snuggled but stopped when Craig was getting close. Storme reached for the specimen cup she'd placed on the nightstand within easy reach. Then she returned her attention to assisting in the process by working him into a frenzy.

"Quick! Get the catcher's cup," Craig groaned.

Storme quickly complied. "Roger that."

Craig played his part, helping to get everything prepared. Storme held the cup as Craig—depleted as he was—readied the syringe, expelling any air before he loaded it. She almost laughed when he flicked it like nurses did before they give someone a shot. He looked at her blazing eyes, and her heart filled with a mixture of love and hope.

He kissed her and embraced her tenderly, then handed her the syringe with its precious cargo. "Go time."

Craig recovered enough to clean up, and when they left the bedroom, he was somewhat red-faced.

Dr. Cyd had arrived as promised, washed her hands, placed her bag nearby, and looked ready to take charge as if this was simply another house call.

Storme handed the syringe to Dr. Cyd and pulled Craig into the guest bedroom, where Sunny lay draped with a clean sheet. Her modesty was protected, and the environment was as sterile as possible. She and Sunny had changed the bedding and cleaned the room that morning. Jesse was standing beside Sunny with a look of concern and worry.

Dr. Cyd walked in and removed a small pillow from the bag she carried, and placed it beneath Sunny's hips, tilting her pelvis to better receive the sperm.

Dr. Cyd glanced around the room as she donned her sterile gloves. "Why am I not surprised you're all crowding in here? Storme, go and wash your hands."

"Already done, doc."

Dr. Cyd nodded and huffed. "Looks like this is a family affair. Jesse, get behind Sunny and support her shoulders."

Sunny sighed as Jesse positioned himself behind her, holding onto her shoulders tenderly to provide moral support. "You're not going to tell me to relax and pretend I'm at the beach, are you?"

Dr. Cyd chuckled. "I never understood that line either. No woman would do that at the beach. Just raise your knees like you're getting a pelvic, and yes, relax as much as possible."

Storme started the playlist on her phone. Paul Anka's *Having My Baby* filled the room and everyone teared up.

Craig stood next to Storme as she held Sunny's hand.

Dr. Cyd raised a brow in question. "Ready?"

Sunny nodded and clutched Storme's hand so tightly she winced. "Should I do a yoga pose like Storme did last summer?"

"No!"

Dr. Cyd had brought her own sterile-wrapped speculum

and used it to open Sunny's vulva. She held the syringe, bent to locate Sunny's cervix, and injected the sperm. "Do your thing, little boys."

She removed the syringe and speculum and closed Sunny's legs, patting her thigh. "That ought to do it. Now lie here for about thirty minutes." She removed her gloves and left the room.

A few moments later, Storme heard the front door as Dr. Cyd quietly let herself out of the house.

Jesse cleared his throat. He was concentrating, judging from the look on his face and the furrows on his forehead. "OMG. If this takes, you could deliver on or around the Fourth of July!"

"Wow, when we got engaged!" Sunny said.

"And saw the Ghost Stag!"

Everyone froze, and then all hell broke loose. There was laughing and crying at the same time. Backslappin', fist pumpin', mutual joyous whoops, and whistles expanded to fill the room.

Like a good patient, Sunny lay still, keeping her excitement to a minimum.

Storme wiped tears from her eyes. Then she looked at each of the others in the room. "Thank you, Sunny, Craig, Jesse. I'll never forget this as long as I live."

When Thanksgiving rolled around, the coronavirus seemed to be in its second wave. Folks were encouraged and then firmly urged to limit their family gatherings. Storme and Sunny had decided their group had formed a COVID-19-free bubble. Not one of them violated the least safety precaution. They maintained social distance, used online orders to bring in groceries, and wore their masks.

Storme was making a small turkey dinner, as were Eve and her new family and her twin sister Dawn with Drew and

Molly.

John and Marsha were eating with Millie and Herman while Skye and her tribe stayed home for their own family dinner.

Storme served non-alcoholic cider in wine goblets, and when they went around the table to say what they were thankful for, she held up her glass and said, "I am thankful for Sunny!"

Sunny raced around the table to hug her. "OMG! I hope it *took*."

A chorus of *me toos* resounded like an echo.

Chapter Fourteen: What a Wonderful World

Sunny felt she was pregnant. She was sure of it. But several days after the injection, she awoke and saw red—literally. "Jesus, Mary, and Joseph, what the hell?"

Panic filled her, and she feared the worst. *Did I jump the gun? Did it fail? Is this my period? How will I tell Storme?* Furiously, she texted Dr. Cyd.

SOS. Spotting? Have I miscarried?

Breathe. I think it's implantation bleeding.

A few minutes later, Sunny's phone was blowing up with messages from Dr. Cyd.

Normal.

Not to worry.

Take a home pregnancy test in a few weeks. Despite the advertisements, they're more reliable after several weeks when the hormones show up more.

And to answer your unasked question . . . Wait a few more days, then you and Jesse can resume normal sexual relations.

Sunny swallowed hard. *Uh-oh, we kinda already did. No one told us not to. Dr. Cyd doesn't need to know that. Nobody does. Right?*

Sunny made a beeline for the Walgreens in Pigeon Forge and bought a pregnancy test kit. When she got home, she wished it was a week later. Now she had to wait like Dr. Cyd told her.

The week dragged on and on. For Sunny, it felt like she'd

been waiting a whole year. Come to think about it, it felt like the rest of 2020 had—endless.

Storme's minute-by-minute barrage of calls, texts, and questions wore on Sunny's nerves. Her tongue would soon get a hole in it, since she'd been biting it, trying not to say something mean that'd she surely would regret. She wanted to send her sister to the moon. *Make that Pluto.* That would give her some relief from constant pestering.

Storme's going nuts. I get how anxious she is, but asking me every five minutes is going to drive me cray-cray. I wish I could block her, but that would be cruel and unusual punishment . . . or torture . . . or something like that, right? Besides, I could still have a period. I'm in the first month, after all. If I am even pregnant, and with that spotting, who really knows?

But it was finally time. Sunny peed on the stick and waited the longest three minutes of her life. Then read the results. She was pregnant! *Thank God! Don't think I'll say anything yet—just in case.*

Storme placed her umpteenth call to Sunny to see if anything different had occurred. "You pukin' yet?"

Sunny ushered a deep sigh. "No."

"Are your nipples tender?"

"No more than usual."

"Did they turn color?"

Sunny snapped. "They're turning red like my anger. Quit it. Stop with all the symptoms. You'll be the first to know."

Storme pouted. "Actually, I'd be the second to know."

"Every day, you are sounding more like me, ya know?"

Storme tried again. "Are you gaining weight?"

"Storme Marie Knight, stop. Right now. Quit asking. Good grief! I know the symptoms, ya know? I'm checking my panties every ten minutes, for God's sake. Cut it out. These things take time. It has to implant and do a whole batch of other stuff. There's some number that has to double or something."

"Have you talked with Cyd?"

"Yes, a million times. She tells me what I tell you. She's the one who told me about the number, but she thinks it's too early to tell."

"Should I call her then? If you think I'm calling too much?"

Storme knew she was pushing too hard, but she couldn't help it. She struggled to control herself. She bit her lip. She wanted to cry. The waiting was terrible. She could tell by Sunny's tone her questions had Sunny on thin ice.

"Sure, if you want to drive her cray-cray, be my guest," Sunny grumbled. "Chill. This is probably why you haven't conceived yet."

Storme tried to be patient, she really did, but the anxiety over the issue had wrung her stomach for weeks. She was feeling nauseous over it. "Okay. I'll try to relax."

Sunny pushed back. "Are you meditating?"

Storme grimaced but remained silent.

"I didn't think so. Go meditate."

Storme agreed and ended the call.

She tried to meditate, but it was hard, because her focus was on babies and Sunny. Images of Sunny's period came to mind. She shook her head to clear it and took a deep breath. *Inhale. Exhale. Inhale . . . I wonder if panting really works during labor? Oops, start over. Inhale, exhale . . . Should I ask Sunny to have a natural childbirth? Isn't childbearing natural? Will she bite my head off if I ask? Am I meditating? I don't think so. This sucks. Can I nurse if I'm not giving birth? Is it fair to ask Sunny to? What if she won't? What if she gets mad? What if she's not pregnant? Meditation is stupid. I can't do it. Is time moving slowly? Or fast? What day is it? Does Sunny have pregnancy brain? Is that why she gets so crazy mad when I ask a simple question? Dang . . . The same thing happens every time I try to meditate. My brain goes hyperactive. It's just not my thing.*

December rolled around. Storme was beside herself, and Sunny had lost patience with her more than once. She didn't blame her. The coronavirus numbers were rising, and they were all suffering from COVID-19 fatigue.

Should they get together for Christmas? How could they not? It would be Christmas soon. *Hell, even the weather is mixed up and messed up like everything else nowadays. It's sixty degrees. It feels like time is not moving at all.*

When Storme wasn't shopping online, she was wrapping Christmas gifts. She wondered if they'd get to open them. She wrote out Christmas cards, did more wrapping, baked the usual sugar cookies in cute holiday cookie cutters, and even made a fruitcake. *I don't even like fruitcake! Does anyone actually eat those things? Mine could double as a doorstop*. She decided to give this one to Sunny.

She called Sunny. *Pick up, pick up.*

Sunny finally answered the call. "Do not ask me a thing. The answer is nothing new."

"I am calling to tell you I made you a fruitcake."

"You're a nut. The only thing around here nuttier than you is a nut. Therefore, logic says you are a nut."

"You are. There's nuts in it, though. You must be psychic."

"Goodbye, Storme." Sunny hung up.

Crabby little bitch. Storme put her hand over her mouth as if she had said that out loud and jinxed herself, or worse, made Sunny mad. Again. *Cancel. Cancel. I didn't mean that.*

At long last, Christmas Eve arrived. The family had decided to play it safe, particularly in case Sunny was pregnant. Storme managed to calm her anxiety a bit and was cuddled with Craig on the sofa when her phone rang.

It was Sunny. "You check under the tree?"

"Not yet. Why?"

"Well, do it and find out. You'll find a little package there."

Craig sat up. "What's going on?"

"I'm supposed to look for a gift from Sunny under the tree."

Storme walked over to the Christmas tree and shuffled through the gifts there. Craig helped move things around. She found a gift trimmed with holly. It was cylindrical. She shook it and swore it fizzled. She opened it. Inside was a can of Mountain Dew. *WTF? Seriously?*

Storme's voice raised in confusion. "You got me a can of Mountain Dew?"

Sunny chirped. "Read the label."

Storme peered at the can and noted it was personalized like Coke was sometimes. It read . . .

Your Mountain due date *is the Fourth of July 2021. For Mama from Your little package.*

Storme's hand flew to her mouth, covering it. She was laughing and crying at the same time. "Truly?"

"Seriously! We're pregnant with your little star!" Sunny assured.

Storme showed Craig the can, and they both jumped for joy!

Craig grabbed her, whirling her around. "Oh, my God!"

"The Ghost Stag or Gram or both have played a hand in this," Storme cried.

It was the best Christmas ever.

Chapter Fifteen: Total Eclipse of the Heart

Storme woke up on Christmas day, smelled the coffee, and bolted for the bathroom. Lord, I hope this isn't COVID-19. Is vomiting a sign of infection or what? No. Can't be.

The smell of the coffee turned her stomach.

I can smell. I must be okay. Maybe it's all the holiday excitement or left-over bile from all the anxiety. To rule it out, Storme took her temperature. *Normal. Whew, that's a relief. Must be a fluke. Maybe sympathy nausea? Twins sharing symptoms?*

She called Sunny and blurted, "Are you experiencing any nausea?"

"Nope. Fit as a fiddle."

"That's because I'm doing it for you."

Sunny hung up.

Two hours later, Sunny called back. "Thanks a lot for sharing. I've been puking ever since you called."

"Must be the twin thing. Although it seems to be working backward."

Sunny's voice rose an octave. "Wait. You don't think it's . . . Oh, God help us, no. Do you . . . do you . . . I can't say it. Let's take our temperature."

"Really, Sunny, you are turning the corner."

"Just do it."

Storme had just taken hers, so she just waited for Sunny.

It took several minutes before Sunny replied. "Normal. Gotta go."

By Valentine's Day, Storme was still having all-day morning sickness.

"Sympathy morning sickness," Sunny always said. "We're predictable. At least as far as sympathy illnesses, pains, and feelings, but you can stop now. Mine has."

"Good. That's a huge relief."

Neither twin had gained an ounce, most likely because all they ever ate was soda crackers. They drank ginger ale by the gallon. Dr. Cyd kept them both supplied.

One day, Dr. Cyd asked Storme over the phone, "Any chance *you* are pregnant?"

Storme held her hand over her heart. Her breathing stopped. "Me? No. Nope. Nada. I got my periods."

"You could be pregnant and still be having your periods. It's not uncommon."

"No. Trust me. All I have is nausea. Haven't gained weight. Breasts the same color, not tender."

"I could do a blood draw."

Storme crossed her fingers as if warding off a werewolf despite the fact Dr. Cyd could not see her. "Needles. My veins take a deep dive even with the suggestion of a blood test. No thank you, ma'am. No need."

"Have it your way."

Storme slowly gained weight, as did Sunny. While Sunny welcomed the gain, Storme held back her complaints. They were both convinced—as was everyone else was—that the weight gain was psychological in origin, manifesting in reality. Storme felt as if she was sharing the pregnancy. *Geesh, now I sound like Mom, all new age and everything. Still, Sunny and I do things together. It happens to one, and the other feels it, too.*

When Sunny felt life and had Storme feel her belly, Storme was positive she was not secretly pregnant.

"Hey, little one," she crooned to Sunny's belly. "Mama here. How's my baby?" Then she planted a million kisses all over Sunny's womb.

"Enough. Stop already," Sunny cried. "You might give me cooties with all that kissin'."

Storme's stomach soon took to gurgling with a movement that she chalked up to drinking a gazillion ounces of ginger ale.

Sunny shook her head and said, "You better call Doctor Quack and see what's cookin'."

Storme giggled at her ob-gyn doctor's nickname, but she was resistant. "I don't want to hear the word *endometritis* again in this lifetime."

Sunny's tone turned stern and commanding. "You are supposed to cater to my merest whim. I'm preggers with your baby. Call, for Gawd's sake."

Storme laughed. "You are getting plenty of mileage out of that *your-wish-is-my-command* thing. Just sayin'."

"Just do it."

Storme placed the call as Sunny watched. She quickly explained the reason for calling and frowned as she listened to the doctor. "Really?" Then she repeated, "Nausea. Weight gain. That's it."

She rummaged through a drawer, found a pen, grabbed the paper, and asked, "How do you spell that?" She repeated each letter as she scrawled. "O-v-a-r-a-i-n. H-y-p-e-r-s-t-i-m-u-l-a-t-i-o-n. What's that?"

The doctor told her.

"Thanks. Bye." She hung up.

She turned to face Sunny. "Happy now?"

Sunny prompted her. "Well, what did he say?"

"Bloating, pain, cramping, and vomiting means I have a condition that mimics pregnancy, but it's only . . . Here, read it for yourself." She thrust the scrawling toward Sunny.

Sunny frowned. "I can't read your penmanship when you write things on a newspaper."

"It was the nearest paper available."

Sunny persisted. "What's all that about bloating?"

"Basically, it's called a pseudopregnancy. Happy now?"

"I just want to err on the safe side. If you were pregnant, you'd need medical care."

"Well, I'm not. Can we change the subject?"

"What, you don't want to talk pregnancy? Since when? Oh . . . I can answer that. Never, that's when."

Storme sighed. "Since my call to . . . what'd you call him?"

Sunny chuckled. "Doctor Quack."

"Yeah, him."

Sunny nodded and smiled. "All in good time. Good things come to those who wait. Think happy thoughts."

"You think happy thoughts," Storme grumbled.

"We're so immature."

"I know, right? We gotta grow up."

"You first."

Epilogue

Spring came and went, and the coronavirus still kept folks on edge. Storme *pseudopregnancy* kept pace with Sunny as summer limped in like, well, like Sunny. Actually, Sunny was waddling . . . and so was Storme. *Seriously this twin sharing thing is getting old. Sunny has had the world's longest pregnancy, and I've been living it with her.*

A summer storm threatened the area, and the barometer fell.

It had begun to rain when Jesse called. "It's go time. Sunny contractions have begun."

"It's not the Fourth of July!" Storme screamed.

In the background, Sunny was yelling, "Jesse Days, get me to the hospital. Now!"

"Meet you two at Mountain Heritage," Jesse blurted, then hung up.

"Craig, it's time. Get the car. The baby's coming!"

Craig heaved her up into his monster truck. They would need the traction and the speed in this storm. Mountain mist was almost a fog, so he had to use the fog lights. The moon was full, giving the scenery an eerie glow.

When they reached the hospital, Sunny was already there. Storme doubled over as Sunny was wheeled into the hospital on a gurney.

Storme glared when an orderly insisted she should use a wheelchair, too. "I'm the mother. I don't need a wheelchair."

The orderly looked confused. "Whatever you say, ma'am, but you surely are pregnant. Look at yourself. Looks like your water broke."

Storme growled in frustration. "I think I peed myself."

The orderly nodded. "That happens, too, during early labor."

"I'm not the pregnant one. My sister is, not me."

"Whatever you say, ma'am."

Storme shook with fury. "Don't you *ma'am* me. I'm too young to be a ma'am." But she gave in. "Take me to my sister. I'm her birth coach."

"You seem to be in transition, ma'am."

Storme just grunted in reply. *Not gonna give that cretin the satisfaction of a response.*

The storm waged on outside. When Storme got to Sunny's room, she leapt from the wheelchair, then doubled over in sympathy pain. Blood gushed from between her legs. *Damn, I'm having my fuckin' period.* She grabbed her belly, experiencing the worst menstrual cramps ever.

Just then, Sunny's water broke, the wind blew hard against the windows, and then amniotic fluid flowed . . . *from Storme.* She bellowed in pain, and the stunned nurse ran to her side. She got her on the nearby gurney that Sunny had just vacated and rushed her out of the room.

The nurse yelled out, "This one's pregnant too! And it looks like she's going to pop it out any second. Get her to delivery. Stat."

Storme made them wait and reached for Sunny's hand. While the wind roared, Sunny gave birth right where she was in the labor room. She had a very white-blonde-haired baby girl.

Two minutes later, after a rush to the delivery room next door, *Storme* gave birth to a dark-haired little girl!

Storme managed a chuckle when she spotted Craig and Jesse, rooted to the floor between the rooms with their jaws hanging open.

Jesse choked out, "What just happened?"

Craig closed his mouth, then spoke. "Hell, if I know."

"Does this mean you have twins?"

Craig fainted.

Storme and Sunny were sharing a room, and both their husbands were present. When things had settled down, they learned that Sunny had been pregnant but with Jesse's baby. Not only was the baby a dead ringer for Jesse, but she also had the female familial webbing between her second and third toe, like all the Days women.

Storme's baby was dark-haired and brown-eyed. Since she was a baby of the mist, they named her Misty.

Craig chuckled. "Misty Knight. Works for me. Goes along with y'all being named after the weather and seasons."

Storme was excited. "Summer can be her middle name. After Sunny. Misty Summer Knight."

Sunny piped up. "We're going to call this one—"

"Windy!" everyone chorused.

Sunny's eyes widened. "How'd y'all know?"

Again in unison, they all sing-songed, "*Everyone knows it's Windy.*"

Jesse laughed. "We knew cuz we know you. Windy Storme Days, she is. Ah has spoken."

Craig grinned. "You sound like Mammy Yokum from the Lil Abner comics strip."

Sunny smiled at Storme. "Told ya so. All you had to do was chillax." She winked. "And slip Skye's magic diaper under the sheets."

Storme smiled down at the baby at her breast and nodded. "We did it. Always did do things together."

The End

Other Books by Kathy Kalmar:

The Beach Series

Beyond the Beach 1
Beyond the Beach 2
Beyond the Beach 3
Beyond the Beach 4
Beyond the Beach 5

Back to the Beach 1
Back to the Beach 2

Promises on the Beach

The Mountain Series

Mountain Hot
Mountain Christmas
Mountain Skye Prequel, The Weather Girls
Mountain Joy
Mountain Kiss
Mountain Holly
Mountain Promises
Mountain Silver
Mountain Mistletoe
Mountain Bred
Mountain Led
Mountain Wed
Mountain Hookup

Mountain Fever
Mountain Due

YOU MAY ALSO ENJOY THE FOLLOWING FROM EXTASY BOOKS INC:

Mountain Fever
Kathy Kalmar

Excerpt

Shit! Fuck! Just when I finally get a chance to get my hair done, a much-needed manicure, and a pedicure, and what happens? Call to Duty! Report to base. Dawn Winters's—make that Second Lieutenant Dawn Winters of the Great State of Tennessee's National Guard—cell phone pinged. It was a text issuing marching orders just as she arrived at Shears Salon, recently re-opened after the Stay Home, Stay Safe order expired.

Off duty, she was a nurse. Things were heating up with a new virus spreading throughout the community like the Chimney Two Wildfire of 2016. Now, she could no longer take the time for grooming. While not a call to battle, she and other medical and military people like her were called to action just as seriously as if they were being deployed for wartime. Today they were fighting another kind of war—the global COVID-19 pandemic.

She had barely pulled into the much-coveted parking spot at Shears Salon with her windows down to breathe the crisp spring Smyrna, Tennessee air. Suddenly, the god-awful screech of metal meeting metal caused her stomach to pitch like a skiff in a storm. Her Volkswagen bug had obviously hit another vehicle.

She smacked her forehead into the steering wheel in frustration, yelling, "Fuck a damn duck!" through the open window. She shoved the gear shift into park and bolted out of her car, ready for combat. There was no time for this. She had places to be, lives to save, a fight to win, and now an accident.

Her body collided with a hunk of an iron-chested giant, who failed to back up enough to permit her to completely assess the situation. He was literally in her face. Well, he would have been in her face had she been a seven-foot-tall Amazon. As it was, all she saw was a black t-shirt stretched tight across a linebacker—with full gear on—massive chest. A torso that wasn't a featherbed.

His tone, when he spoke, came out in a lazy drawl. "Whoa, Nelly, don't get your panties in a twist, lady. Who taught you to drive? A snowplow driver? And who taught that pretty little mouth to talk so ugly?"

Not one to stay quiet, she didn't miss a beat. "My imaginary seafaring father taught me his colorful language, and my football coach taught me to drive," she ground out. "Did your granny teach you?"

The cad took her by the shoulders and moved her backward, providing much-needed space and relief from those rock-hard abs and hard chest. "How 'bout we take a look-see and figure out how much you owe me for ramming that red M&M into my truck?"

"You mean tank, don't you? That's no truck." The thing rested on huge wheels. "Is it legal to even drive that thing on the streets? That's a King Kong of a vehicle. And I think you crushed my bug. You owe me, mister."

The jerk met her rants with a loud guffaw. "Little spitfire, aren't ya?"

She fumed and blew the hair that had fallen from her

messy top bun out of her eyes. "Don't you patronize me. Give me your insurance info, and let's get this over with. I'm late. I need your phone, so I can sync my data. Be sure to include your insurance company, too."

He handed it to her with a half-grin, steered her backward, and took a long look. "Not even a fender-bender, but I can't say the same for your VW. Why don't you call your insurance company, and I'll get you to where you're in such a hurry to go. Name's Drew Sunrise, by the way." He looked at his phone and her contact data. "Dawn is it? But tell me, where in tarnation is the frickin' fire?"

Her temper fumed. "It's Second Lieutenant Winters to you. If you must know, I've been called to active duty. That's why I'm in such a rush."

He whistled at her declaration. "A duty call." He chuckled.

"Beats a booty call," she said and then felt her face flame. Oh no, I did not just say that out loud, did I?

He cocked a brow in her direction. "Seriously? I doubt that."

She bit back a smile and nodded. "The power of a syringe in my hand can't be matched."

He winked. "Wanna bet?"

She nodded. "I've seen grown men faint at the sight of a needle."

"Don't you mean gun?"

"Nope. I'm a nurse practitioner with the National Guard. Some folks don't like shots."

"I like 'em, all right. 'Specially if they're Tequila."

Dawn bit back a laugh.

He grew serious. "You're being called in to fight the coronavirus?"

"I am."

"Thank you for your service. That takes guts. Look, it doesn't matter who's at fault here. You have a job to do and no wheels. Let me get you where you need to go. It's only fair, and this mop and fuzz can go a few more days without a trim."

She took a close look at him, and what met her eyes was all but stunning. He was one hot dude. His hair was now being secured into a low dark brown ponytail, while his face wore a kinda sexy stubble on its way to becoming a beard. Chocolate eyes smiled at her, the crowfeet beside them only highlighting his gotta be fifty-something years. A quick glance at his ring finger revealed no telling gold band or pale skin from one being recently removed.

Seeing no choice but to take him up on his offer, she shook off her false pride and attitude and followed his advice.

Her bug looked smashed. Its engine hissed, leaked, and smoked. She took photos of the damage to send to the insurance company while noting his truck had nary a scratch. The impact didn't even appear to reach his bumper. She just hoped her claim would be filed as easily as the television ads promised.

She stretched a leg up to climb into his truck when he opened the door. She didn't make it all the way and fell back into him. His hand shot upward, catching her by her butt, guiding her in safely.

Surprisingly, Dawn liked the tingle caused by the heat of his hand on her fanny, but she didn't enjoy the fact that she liked it a little too much. More than glad for her fit body, she applauded her workouts to an old program, Buns of Steel.

She flashed him a smirk. "I bet you thought I was just a pretty face going for a facial."

He laughed. "Well, you are fragile, sugar."

Before she could detonate, he held up his hands in surrender, shut the door, and circled the vehicle.

Once behind the wheel, he elaborated, "Not delicate like a flower, but more like a bomb is fragile. Handle with care and use extreme caution."

She relaxed and retracted her claws, happy she managed to bite her tongue.

"No, not when you flew into me like a bat from hell. I knew

for sure, you got grit beneath your mop of curls. Reminds me of a cute black poodle."

She groaned. "Great, just what every woman wants to hear."

He laughed as she gave him the address and pointed out where he needed to drive.

"What? You don't like poodles?"

"Cute. No woman wants to be cute."

He glanced at her, his reply cautious. "I was afraid to say hot. You being a female Second Lieutenant and all."

She agreed. "Yeah, dems fightin' words for sure."

He eyed her carefully. "You a libber?"

She stared at him. "A libber? What the hell is that?"

"A Woman's Liberation Movement uh . . . woman . . . Er . . . person."

She laughed, and her voice rose an octave. "Women's Lib? Holy cow. That's an old one. How old are you anyway?"

"Old enough." He slid a glance in her direction. "You don't sound like you're from here."

She smiled for the first time since literally bumping into him. "I'm not. What gave me away?"

"Your accent."

She gave a big belly laugh." Really? My accent? Mr. Southern Dude."

He tried again. "You're not from here. Obviously. Where y'all from?"

"Sunny California."

He slapped his forehead. "That's a long sight from here."

"I'm visiting my friend, Marie, and using my twin sister's place until I decide where I might settle next." She looked at him sideways. "You live here?"

"Nope. Live about three hours east. Just here meeting with a consultant, and it's back home to Molly I go."

"Turn here." Who's Molly? He wears no ring. Why do I care? I'm not gonna marry him! For all I know, Molly is his pet gerbil. Or goldfish. I don't think I'd give him custody of my cactus. Maybe Molly's a dog . . . a basset hound. That sounds about right.

He smiled. "I got it. GPS." You have reached your destination sounded from the dashboard. "See?"

She thanked him as she moved to get out, declaring she could fend for herself and get a ride.

"Look, I got nuthin' else goin' on. You have no wheels. How about I drive you to the base?" He looked contrite.

"I can take an Uber." He's trying to make amends. Give him a chance. He's hardly a serial killer. "Look, you don't owe me anything. All I need to do is grab my go bag."

"That's a thing? Really."

She winked. "It is, and it's ready. I'll just be a second."

When she accepted his help out of the truck, she couldn't miss the jolt of electricity igniting her insides. Uh-oh. After she dug out her key. After she unlocked the door. After she donned her fatigues. After she watered her lone cactus. After she grabbed her twin sisters' computer. After she thanked God that she had no kids dependent on her, let alone a spouse to inform. She finally hefted her duffle bag, retrieved an extra facemask, closed the blinds, locked up, and—with a mental kick in her ass—accepted Drew's offer and used his help to get back into the truck.

"Here." She handed him a face mask emblazoned with the American flag.

"What's this?"

"My peace offering. I came off like a bitch on wheels—literally. You're going to need this. Especially since my orders are directly related to the surge in coronavirus numbers."

"Aww. Ain't that sweet. Didn't know you cared."

"Get over yourself. It's just a mask."

He grew serious. "No, it's PPE, and it's already damn hard to get. Thank you."

"That's my line."

"Truce," he said, holding out his hand.

She took it, felt the zap of heat, and replied, "Truce."

About the Author

Kathy Kalmar, born in Detroit, Michigan, lives with Larry, her husband of four decades. Lately, she feels her life has recovered from the bad country song-like life because her Smoky Mountain Tops Round House is now rebuilt from the 2016 Chimney Tops II Wildfire. Her current residence is enlarged by four feet with the addition of their new puppy, Valentina. She loves to read and write contemporary romance novels. Meanwhile she remains fond of hot tubbing, chocolate, and sipping wine, mai tais and moonshine whether at home, Waikiki, Cape Cod or Tennessee. Y'all come back, hear? Currently, she is writing her next book. Aloha and Mahalo.

Contact Kathy at KathyKalmar.com

www.ingramcontent.com/pod-product-compliance
Lightning Source LLC
Chambersburg PA
CBHW070508130626
46555CB00003B/1199
9781487432454